THE FATMAN, THE SWORD-BEARER, AND THE WELL-WOMAN

CONVERSATIONS WITH THE VOICES IN MY HEAD

BY CAMI OSTMAN

THE FATMAN, THE SWORD-BEARER, AND THE WELL-WOMAN

CONVERSATIONS WITH THE VOICES IN MY HEAD

CAMI OSTMAN

Sidekick Press
Bellingham, Washington

Publisher's Note: Portions of this work are memoir. Names, characters, places, and incidents are products of the authors' recollections. Some names of individuals have been changed. Locales and public names are sometimes used for atmospheric purposes. Any resemblance to actual people, living or dead, or to businesses, companies, events, institutions, or locales is completely coincidental. Fictional pieces in this anthology reflect the imaginations of the authors. Each individual author is responsible for the content of their work.

Sidekick Press
2950 Newmarket Street
Suite 101-329
Bellingham, Washington 98226
www.sidekickpress.com

The Fat Man, The Sword-Bearer, and The Well-Woman
ISBN 978-1-958808-02-3
LCCN 2022915496

Cover Design: Spoken Design

DEDICATION

To my writing students, whose stories matter more to me than I can say. May you make peace with all the parts of yourself so you can reach those who need to hear what you have to say.

INTRODUCTION

I never meant to publish the three weird little stories in this book. I wrote them for my own therapeutic reasons—many years ago. In fact, these stories are more than two decades old, and when I read them now, I feel both deep compassion for the young woman who experienced and wrote them and a little embarrassed at how formal and dramatic I was back then, even in the privacy of my own journals. (Note: inner critics are real!)

Over the years, only a handful of people have seen these three pieces, always because I believed reading about *my* journey would help the person I gave them to—never because I wanted to make these writings public.

You see, before I was an author and certainly before I founded The Narrative Project (my program for writers giving them everything they need to get their books done), I had several people-helping careers. I worked as an educator in public schools and at universities, I was a program director for a social work agency, and I was a family therapist for twenty years per my training in my master's program. All the while, no matter what venue I was working in, the number one struggle I saw people grappling with was against their inner critics. When, after the publication of my own first two books, I began working with writers as an editor and writing coach, the refrain I heard constantly was, "I can't write this book because . . ." You could finish that sentence with a million self-sabotaging statements—anything from, "I have laundry to do," to, "My family will never speak to me again."

Once I launched my first nine-month group coaching program for writers—which includes classes, critique groups, one-on-one coaching, and massive doses of structure, support, and accountability—to help them complete their books, I knew that helping would-be authors with the negative voices in their heads would be crucial and of priority. After all, what stops us from doing many, if not most things we truly want to do is negative mindset, false beliefs, and poor self-talk.

I knew if I wanted to help writers complete their manuscripts, I'd have to help them first with what was happening between their ears. So, I created a six-week deep-dive class on the inner critic, putting to use what I knew about how to manage my own inner saboteurs and offering the techniques I'd used in working with therapy clients.

One of the most effective things we do in the inner critic course is what I call "an interview with a part." This is an opportunity for a sabotaging part of the self to have its say, to be deeply understood, and to interact directly with the "core self" of the writer in an effort to bring greater internal harmony. The technique for the interview I created is a hybrid from interventions offered by two therapy theories I quite like: the "parts work" of a theory called Internal Family Systems and the "externalization" process used in Narrative Therapy.

The interview exercise is wildly popular among the writers who work with us in The Narrative Project's nine-month programs because people routinely experience lasting shifts in terms of their negative self-talk after participating in an interview with their inner critic. And these shifts give them permission to write their authentic stories!

The "interview with a critic" technique originally emerged out of an experience I had privately. Back in graduate school, I wrote a story on a lark to help me deal with my own life-long, debilitating, generalized anxiety. While working on my graduate thesis, I found perfectionism was baring down on me so intensely, I was paralyzed and couldn't write anything cohesive at all. One morning, with my deadline pressing in, I sat down in my little rented house to journal about my stuckness, and what poured out of me was a full story about the history of my relationship with anxiety. What a relief it was to finally be able to talk directly to this ever-present, plaguing saboteur who was now threatening to keep me from being able to complete my education.

When I got up from writing that story many hours later, I was almost miraculously freed up from the energy of perfectionism. I went to bed, had a good night's sleep, and got up in the morning to work on my thesis.

And that particular perfectionistic anxiety has never plagued me again!

I'm not kidding. Ask anyone who knows me. I'm not perfect, and I don't mind at all.

I've continued to use what I spontaneously learned with that first story about anxiety—that I could talk (and listen) to different parts of myself and create real shifts in my way of being in the world by understanding those parts—as a way of becoming freer and freer in my creativity.

Over these past few years, as I've taught the interview exercise to others and talked about how doing the exercise myself had led to writing additional stories about other parts of myself, my writing clients have asked if they could see some of my stories.

As I mentioned, I've shared them occasionally but have always done so reluctantly—because they are extremely vulnerable and intimate. They really represent my own personal journey as opposed to representing narrative writing designed for public consumption.

But one day recently, I realized that my reluctance to share this writing was, in fact, informed by an inner critic—a part that wants to protect me from embarrassment. A part that silences me as a way of keeping me safe from judging eyes. And because I practice what I preach, whenever I notice a part of myself holding me back from being seen and known more fully by other people, I know I have some work to do to help that part calm down and feel safer in the world.

After an internal conversation with my silencing part, I realized I MUST share these stories so that the writers in my community (and others who find their way to this little book) can see deeply inside of how the shift from self-editing to free expression can happen—how we can truly calm and heal activated, terrified parts of ourselves and let the core self shine.

So here is what you hold in your hand in this small volume: The first story in this book is that initial effort at working with an inner critic which spontaneously arose during the writing of my graduate thesis. It is called "The Fat Man." As I said, even as it came time for me to write my final project for my master's program, I was panic ridden and fearful of screwing up—afraid my professors would lose respect for me if I didn't turn in a perfect document. The morning I sat down to face this anxiety—thinking of it as a "part" of my psyche that had split off to manage me (using rather unkind tactics, mind you) in order to keep me safe— I found that I really needed to be able to *see* the character of the anxiety in order to deal with it directly. I closed my eyes to conjure an image of anxiety, and there he was.

In "The Fat Man" story, anxiety, as a heavy person who sometimes sits on my chest, comes to life, which allows me to make changes in my relationship with it (or him). Because the story gave me such a great example of both Internal Family Systems parts work and the Narrative Therapy externalization strategies, I actually cleaned it up and turned it in as part of my thesis to discuss the differences in the theories.

The second story in this little collection, "The Sword-Bearer," is a story I've only recently put on paper (you will see the difference in the writing style from the other two pieces—which were written when I was in my early thirties). It is about a part of myself I have actively worked with for many years (I'm in my 50s at this writing). The Sword-Bearer is what is known in Internal Family Systems as an "exile." She is the part of me who carries the burden of constant "watching." While the Fat Man was a "manager," that is to say, a part of me whose job it was to keep me safe when I was a young, vulnerable child, the Sword-Bearer does not have a job. She is a part that was pushed away when things were unsafe for me as a little girl. She got stuck at about age eight (the age when my parents divorced, incidentally), and she was not allowed expression. In Internal Family Systems work, an inner critic (also called a saboteur or a manager) has a *job*, whereas an exile has a *burden*. Therefore, the Sword-Bearer represents the care-free spirit that, for me, was squashed when I had to take on parentified duties to keep my brothers and myself fed and clothed. Writing her story revolutionized my sense of joy and playfulness. I hope as you read her words and her vision of freedom, you will hear the call of your own exiled parts and that you will go to them, heal them, and set them free!

The third kind of part Internal Family Systems talks about is the "core self," also sometimes called an "inner champion." The last story in this collection is an inner champion story. It is called "Ode to the Well-Woman's Catalyst." This story is about an experience I had with a man (I call him "Adam" here) in my life seeing—I mean REALLY seeing—the me I knew I could be but that I could not access with manager parts activated and leading the way. She was "there" all along, and once I did the work with the Fat Man, the Well-Woman's voice became eminent in my internal "system" (my psyche). That is to say, the badass voice of the Well-Woman, the voice that always has my back completely and carries deep wisdom for my life, is more often than not the first voice I now hear in my head when walking about in the world on a daily basis.

Dear Reader, we are multi-faceted, complex, nuanced creatures. The parts (or subpersonalities—or narratives, if you will) I've explored in these stories have given me language and images for my lived experience of anxiety, smallness, and emerging strength, respectively. Living these stories and writing them in the first place has set me free to live a life of joy, audacity, and abundance. Although I publish them here specifically for students of The Narrative Project who have asked to see them, I hope they will help any and all readers connect to their own parts in meaningful ways. If they do, they've done even better work than I could have hoped for.

Enjoy what you read in these pages. And then wonder, engage with, and write of and for your own parts, Dear One. And if you want extra support to engage by using the "Interview with a Part" exercise, you can find the information about the Inner Critic Relief class at: https://thenarrativeproject.net

Go forth with freedom and speak/write your truths.

Your Story Warrior,
Cami

THE FATMAN

NOTE: Although I no longer grapple with the particular perfectionistic anxiety of the Fat Man, I am resurrecting this story for you, reader, because the story is a solid example of how Inner Critic conversations can work to set people free. The Fat Man story shows how parts of us emerge (often quite early in our lives), how they work hard to keep us safe, and how they ultimately don't know they have lost their functionality once the threat of harm is dispensed with. The Fat Man story shows how we can work to set them free from the tactics they engage.

Be kind but firm as you work with your own inner saboteurs. They are tenacious for a reason, but they are usually willing to be convinced to move on when they know we are strong enough to manage life without them.

When my mother gave birth to me, along with the placenta, she pushed out a tiny little Fat Man. I later discovered that each of the women in my family had a Fat Man of their own. My mother had one. My grandmother had one too—still does. I have seen him, or results of Grandma's relationship with him, in the trenches of the lines in her aging, silken skin. There isn't a woman in my family who doesn't have a Fat Man in her reserve, driving her life. I recall the first time I noticed my dear grandmother's Fat Man. It was Christmas Eve when I was twelve.

She was preparing her famous baked beans recipe in the kitchen when I arrived. There was still much to be done for the holiday dinner. My grandfather was watching television in the other room with one eye and reading a Louis L'Amour western with the other. Even as I came through the front door and embraced her, I sensed a strangely forced attribute in her hug. (My Fat Man encourages the use of empathetic intuition at all times, by the way.) She avoided my eyes and with her hand batted away some dust or phantom beside my head before turning back to her cooking. I inquired how she was and asked if I could help. She smiled a tight-lipped grin which lacked the warmth I was accustomed to. "I'm fine. Go keep your grandfather company."

Alarmed by her odd manner, I wandered into the rec room and greeted Grandpa. No tension there. What could be wrong? When my mother arrived, I asked her if she noticed anything amiss with her own mother. "This is how she was during so much of my childhood," she said. "She would go for two days without speaking, and I would never know what I had done. She never said she was angry at me. Just lived in her own world. The best thing to do is ignore her mood. It goes away quickly nowadays." So I did my best to set my mind toward ignorance, but I had never seen Grandma like this before, and it bothered me. She always seemed so happy at her seldom-ceasing housework, tranquil and steady. She was the most reliable member of my immense extended family. I was terribly unnerved to see her visibly manage some kind of displeasure or frustration. But my mother had told us about strange bouts with paranoid, dissociative symptoms Grandma used to exhibit when Mom was a girl. I had never believed it before. This day, however, I clearly saw her struggling with her Fat Man. The vile bloke was winning. I mistakenly conjectured that if she kept her cool, that would mean she would have won the battle. It would be a long time before I would realize that losing her cool would have been her victory.

As for me, before I even knew I had been begotten into such a tradition of fat men, I was betrothed, promised, sold, as it were, into a relationship from which it would prove very difficult to escape. Had I been warned what my Fat Man would become to me, I certainly would have pleaded to be spared the life of a child-bride. I might have asked to be placed in a different family. Or I might have rap-rapped on the wall of my mother's uterine warmth and asked that she kill her own Fat Man before she pushed me into the world.

I, myself, have never purposely killed anything or anyone before, except for one time, many summers ago when, sunbathing in my front yard, I sliced a bothersome bee in half with the edge of a hard-covered book I was reading. After this murderous act, I was so struck in my conscience that I arose, leaving beach towel and book behind, entered my house, knelt at the edge of my futon sofa and sincerely repented that I had taken the life of an unwitting creature. It was not my right. But do I *not* have the right to kill the Fat Man? He belongs to me as much as I belong to him, yes? Not that I would claim him in any honorable or loving sense, and yet my affair with him has, for many years, been consensual.

He started it, coming into being without any permission from anyone, but I have carried it on, at times.

An early encounter with my Fat Man occurred during one of my parents' innumerable altercations when I was five. Though by no means can I remember the reason for their argument, I shall never forget the experience as a whole. Such chaotic noise and thrashings were common in our home. This particular day was only more startling than others because of the mess it created. The yelling had been carrying on for more than an hour; it was my mother who always became loud. My father incited her by calmly repeating the phrase, "Yes dear," in broken-record style. As he grew more reticent to participate and more passively needling, my mother became more determined to draw him into dispute. My father was not easily swayed, however; he had abnormally adept deflecting skills. The fight moved into the kitchen and, perhaps before *she* even knew what she was about to do, I could see the weapon of my mother's warfare sitting on the dining table, lukewarm and placid. Before the understanding of what was happening fully swept through my young mind, Mother had the milk in her hand, a full glass, left over from breakfast. *Whoosh!* It sailed through the air in the direction of my father's head.

As I said, hurling objects was a common activity in our home, but the splashing of milk on the wall behind my dad startled us all. I was frightened, but there wasn't time to indulge my fear. As if from the air, I heard the Fat Man, who was considerably smaller then than in recent years (rather more "plump" than fat, let's say) speak words of action in my ear. *Don't cry, you little brat. Look around you. Your brothers are frightened and they're smaller than you are. Take them upstairs, then stop the fighting.* He was right, of course. It wouldn't do to cry. I'd been berated by both Mom and Dad the other day for losing control during a scuffle that had ensued between the two of them in the car on the way to Jack-in-the-Box. When they had turned the car around before reaching our destination because they could not stop their fighting, I had started to sniffle, and they had turned their wrath on me. I knew better this time. Better to be useful and decisive than to appear confused or afraid.

I took the boys upstairs and retreated in thought until I came up with the idea to go into the fray and propose a game, the details of which I can no longer recall. Through this strategy, I could surely call a cease-fire in the arguing. If I won the game, I imagined, Mom and Dad would have to stop fighting. I scurried into the kitchen to aptly present the rules to the warriors. My peace-keeping mission would not fail. This house was the foreign field, and I was the grand and proud United States butting in on a mission of my own determination. Unfortunately, my parents wouldn't sign the treaty. As I reached the war zone, I witnessed my father taking a nearly full carton of milk out of the refrigerator and chasing my mother into the basement. She had finally gotten a rise out of him. I returned to my brothers. The Fat Man was repeating in my ear, *Just think what to do next. Don't cry. Don't cry. Don't cry.*

That day, my little plump man grew just a bit.

In the years that passed between that early memory and the day I discovered my grandmother fighting against her Fat Man, my parents divorced. I must admit, I gratefully remember the peace in our home after my father's departure and had never really hoped for a reconciliation between the warring factions as some of my friends have reported they felt after their parents' divorces. I was always glad for the separation. Sometimes borders bring an end to the battles. But alas, my mother married again and guerrilla warfare overtook us.

The Fat Man grew a great deal during this time. As I entered puberty, he grew to his full height and weight. My mother had another child, but, entrenched in her marital problems, the care of the baby was left to me. I wanted to love this tiny brother, but the Fat Man made it very difficult. There was so much to be done, and I didn't know how to care for a baby. I found it very hard to keep my equilibrium and nearly lost my temper with my mother on many occasions. But only "nearly." *Be calm. There is enough rage and passion in this household. Do you want to have the consequences of throwing a tantrum or mouthing off?* the Fat Man advised me. Mouthing off was strictly forbidden.

I longed to break free. I longed to go out with my seventh-grade friends, to skate the trio with Scott Rodriguez holding onto one hand and who-cares-who-else on the other side with "Reunited" playing over the speakers. But my trio and the Fat Man would make four. It's particularly difficult to skate with four. *There's too much to be done at home. Who will take care of the boys? What if your mother and her husband begin to fight? Hadn't you better stay in the house?*

Soon, he was becoming bigger than I. I came to need some relief from his barbarian tactics. I tried Jesus. I had heard that Christ was on my side, and so I walked down the aisle to the alter one Sunday at a little Baptist church in my neighborhood, and perhaps for a while after that, there was a kind of reprieve. All too soon, however, the Fat Man returned from his dormancy with incomparable dominance. He seemed to gain strength in the fact that I was embracing a religious way of life. It was another domain for him to conquer.

I began to go to church, and there I found a family of others who were trying to be saved from something. But the Fat Man must have been jealous of my new-found connections, because before my acquaintance with Jesus was more than one year old, I began to hear that gurgling, demanding voice I had become so familiar with over the years. I heard him when I read the Bible, and I heard him in the church, itself. *Women should not speak in church. Submit. Be humble. Don't be anxious about anything. Go the extra mile. You can do all things through Christ who strengthens you.* I was confused. How could I do all things, yet not be allowed to speak in church? What if I had something to say? I decided to speak to the pastor.

Wednesday morning, I knocked on his door.

"Cami, come in." It was a small church. Pastor F. knew all his parishioners. "What can I do for you?"

I didn't think I should mention the Fat Man. It sounded a little crazy. I'd wait to see what his responses to me would be like. I'd rely on my ever-true intuition. If he seemed to like me, to approve of my attempts at being a good Christian, I might broach what was really bothering me. If he seemed displeased with my efforts, I would make light conversation and hastily say my good-byes.

"I've been wondering about something."

"Certainly, you're a baby Christian. Anything at all."

"Well, it's this thing about women in the church you talked about last Sunday."

"Yes."

"You said that women could teach only women. You said that women should dress in a feminine, becoming way but not a sensual, overly ornate way." I had my notes from Sunday's sermon which I consulted for his precise words.

"Yes."

"What if I have something to say when the men are in the room? Or what if I like to where jeans and sweatshirts instead of skirts and blouses?"

His eyes were very kindly. He looked at me for a moment before he spoke. "How old are you, dear?"

"Fourteen and a half," I answered.

"Well, this is an important time for you to become a lady. Let me put you in touch with one of the women in the church who can mentor you through this difficult time."

That seemed nice. I didn't sense any disapproval. Perhaps a touch of condescension, but that was to be expected; I was a young girl, after all. He was a pastor. I thought I might bring up the Fat Man in a circular manner.

"Is there anything else?"

"Yes. There is something else."

"What is it, dear?"

"Well, I have these thoughts. I get bad feelings from things I think, and I don't know what to do about it." I wanted to say more, but Pastor F was nodding vigorously. I thought, perhaps, he knew all about the Fat Man. Maybe he had one or maybe his wife had one. Maybe all women had them, but I'd just never been told. I looked up at him expectantly.

"It's the devil," he said, still nodding.

"It is?"

"Absolutely!" He was so emphatic. I thought he must know what he was talking about. "The devil is always picking on new Christians. You have to rebuke him."

"But I had these kinds of thoughts before I was a Christian, too." I was slightly doubtful, but I didn't want to appear disrespectful.

"Well, the devil first tries to keep you from Christ, and then when you come, he tries to get you back."

"But my upsetting thoughts don't always have to do with God."

"Well, trust me, Cami. It's the devil. Rebuke him. Rebuke him until it goes away. Do it louder and faster if you have to. Drown him out. You must rebuke him."

"Okay. I will." I stood up quickly. I wanted to get home and look up the word "rebuke" before the Fat Man started in, drowning out this good advice, but Pastor F stopped me. He came out from behind his desk and took my hand, looking into my eyes, gravely.

"One more thing, dear. Some thoughts which bring guilt come from God. You have to discern which is which. Discern. Then, when appropriate, rebuke."

"Discern and rebuke?" I questioned.

"Yes."

"Thank you." I walked home briskly, repeating, "Discern, rebuke, discern, rebuke, discern, rebuke." I didn't want to forget the words before Webster and I could consult.

Oddly enough, although the dictionary never fully explicated the ideas of discerning and rebuking to my complete satisfaction, the Fat Man took them on like a mantra. If I couldn't figure out when a thought was from God or the devil he spoke to me. *All you have to do is discern. What can be so difficult about that? Look in the Bible. What does it say? Be careful not to rebuke guilt that is from God, though. That kind of guilt is your friend, guiding you to right action.*

By now you have the idea. The Fat Man drove me into a heated race to meet every deadline, perform every act perfectly and behave and act and think appropriately in any and all situations. Imperfection of any kind was not tolerated. Any small mistake would bring about a berating I could barely stand under. I would lie in bed stifling the desire to cry after the smallest mishap, the Fat Man's harsh words and warnings of what might happen as a result of my blunders echoing in the continually growing canyon of my heart. The crazy thing is that I listened to him almost gratefully, thinking that perhaps he would drive me to be a good soldier in the Kingdom. I was at war, after all.

After I graduated from high school, the full-time job I landed was boring and the hours dragged. I heard him chiding me for the dead-end position in which I found myself. I worked at a religious bookstore, but constantly found books which ground me into bits with exhortations regarding the laws of religious life. I came up short at every bookshelf. From A to G there were interpretations of the rules on Adultery to Gossip. At W there was the issue of women's behavior and the best ways to be feminine. I didn't measure up, especially on the latter issue. I never intended to get married and have children, but apparently, submitting to one's husband and staying home to raise children was the only life to have if a woman wanted to dignify her existence. I disagreed, but there was no place to say so, and it was risky—akin to disagreeing with God.

I became frightened I might have a life like my mother lived (it would be a long time before I learned that this is a fear many women share). She had had two marriages. In the first, she was angry, tired, and disappointed with a man (my father) who stonewalled her much of the time. In the second, she was submissive, giving over dignity, it seemed to me, in exchange for fending off loneliness.

Submission. It wasn't for me, even though by now I was aware of the condemnation from the Fat Man I might accrue in dispensing with it. I went to college, at first, to postpone submission—and of course, to become the perfect student.

It wasn't until after I had graduated and accepted my first professional job that I noticed the Fat Man was *standing on my chest.* Submission came strongly into play in this new arena, as I had anticipated it. My boss was a man who believed in it. I remember my first disagreement with him. He stepped into my office at 8:10 one morning.

"It's very important that we have coverage in the office right at eight o'clock. Students may need assistance and we've got to make sure the student services coordinator is available. That would be you."

"I'm here."

"You just arrived."

"Mr. M, I worked with the students until ten o'clock last night. I put in twelve hours yesterday. I truly doubt the students will be up this early anyhow." I didn't want to seem disrespectful, but this was a very busy time in the program. I thought it was only fair to be cut some slack about my hours. I didn't get compensation for extra time put in.

"Well, we can't compromise on the office hours. They are posted as eight to four thirty. We've got to keep them."

If you continue to argue, you will lose his good opinion. You did agree to keep those hours. Someday he will write your letter of recommendation. As a Christian, you should submit to authority. If it is unreasonable, leave it to God. I couldn't get a breath. I twisted my shoulders to the left to loosen up my lungs, but no air seeped in.

A fair number of such confrontations occurred during those first years of my professional life. But also, I did get married during this time (against my better judgment, but there was no other way to have sex) and added rules of nuptial appropriateness to the repertoire of demands weighing on me. Eventually, clipped, tense pains bolted through my back and chest daily. I called my physician and asked her to listen to my lungs and heart. I was becoming convinced something was amiss. She examined me, pronounced me healthy and referred me to a therapist.

I marched into my first therapy session, determined to kill the blasted beast, who was by this time, growing more obese each day. Awakening in the mornings and attempting to rise out of my bed had become nearly impossible; my chest was so heavy with his sniggering and jiggling. I sat down in the chair opposite Ms. T, my new therapist.

"I've got a Fat Man on my chest. I can't breathe," I started, desiring that no time be wasted on fishing around when I knew exactly what the problem was.

"Can you tell me more?" She didn't seem surprised at my proclaiming there was a man in the room she couldn't see.

So I continued. "I can only tell you that this ugly man is larger than you and I put together, and he is standing, sometimes jumping, on my chest. I can't get any air."

"Mm hmm. Go on." She jotted down something in her notes.

"There's nothing more to tell," I said, then proceeded for fifty minutes, blabbering on about my family, my job, and my young but already-troubled marriage. At the end of that time, careful not to utilize a moment more than I was about to pay for, I got out my checkbook.

While I scribbled, Ms. T, asked me a final question. "What do you feed this man on your chest?"

I was puzzled. "Feed him?"

"Yes. What do you feed him?"

"Well, I don't feed him at all. He feeds on me."

"So you feed him your 'self,' then?"

I was irritated at the implication that I was in some way participating in the process of his continued fattening.

"No. He eats at his leisure. I don't feed him. He takes what he wants as he pleases."

"Really? Okay. Well, I will see you next week." She stood up, took my check, and shook my hand, dislodging me from the chair where I sat dumbfounded.

"Yeah, sure." I managed.

Walking out into the gray day, I felt lighter. I drew in a breath and the air went all the way to the pit of my lungs. *I'm free*, I thought. Maybe this Fat Man is dead. Maybe all that was needed was for me to confess to someone his existence. He is gone. I was ecstatic at the possibility. Another breath, deep and open. Nearly skipping, I headed toward my little blue Honda Accord. One step before reaching the parking slot, the notion hit me: *You certainly spoke poorly of your mother and your husband. Rather like gossip, don't you think? Somewhat disloyal!* The thought was so clear; it was nearly audible. Yes, I had spoken angrily, almost bitterly, and bitterness is a sin, no doubt. I drew in a breath with the anxiety. No air. He was returned to me, that damned Fat Man.

I reached the car, hastily opening the door and climbing in. When the latch clicked, I grasped for the steering wheel. Suddenly something seemed to overtake me, and an unfamiliar scream broke forth, "Get off me. Get away. Get off my chest and let me breathe. Fuck you! Fuck you! Get away from me." And on and on I yelled until my screaming turned to sobs. I heard him in the background. *You're losing control. Christians shouldn't lose control. Women shouldn't lose control. They should be gentle and giving and placating. Get hold of yourself. Be sensible. Be responsible.* His voice was like the condescending math teacher I had had in the twelfth grade: "I've explained it to you seven times. Perhaps you're not ready for this level yet." Low and steady, but oozing with oily scorn.

"Screw you," I sobbed, my voice already becoming raspy and hoarse.

Again, inappropriate! he said.

I looked up briefly and saw a woman passing by the car in the parking lot. She looked at me, concerned. She was coming toward me. Dear God, I thought, I can't talk to anyone. Still, it wouldn't do to be rude so I unrolled my window.

"Are you all right, dear?" She was a kind-eyed, gray-haired woman, sixtyish. I didn't want to hurt her feelings or make a further fool of myself, but suddenly I wasn't able to lie to her.

"Does it look like I'm okay lady?" The decibel of my voice was rising. "What do think is going on here? Does it look like I'm putting my make-up on for a job interview, or something? I'm having a nervous breakdown. Can't you see I've got an ugly, obese man on my chest? He's trying to kill me. I'm being dismembered, rent to pieces, and you're asking me if I'm okay? You've got to be kidding me. Leave me alone, will you?" And I rolled up my window. The poor woman scurried away toward the clinic.

That was unseemly, I heard.

I *had* been unseemly. That dear woman was trying to be kind, and I had been absolutely unmanageable. I realized I had better apologize before she got out of range. Quickly, I started my car and pulled out of my parking space, racing in the direction of the woman, who was almost at the door of the offices. She must have heard my engine, for she turned around abruptly, and I thought I saw fear in her eyes. I stuck my head out the window and half sobbing, half smiling I said, "Lady, I'm sorry I yelled at you. It wasn't very nice of me." Then I sped away. In my rear-view mirror, I saw her quicken her pace until she reached the building.

It came to me that she might have gotten my license number. In only a moment, I visualized the ambulance coming after me and the EMTs taking me in a straitjacket to the psychiatric wing of the city hospital. I imagined myself in a white room, free of anything that might resemble a weapon of self-destruction, sitting on a bed, writhing to get a full breath of air with no hands free to wipe away the tears draining from my tightly shut eyes, which would be swollen from my uncontrollable sobbing. I imagined being sedated when my husband came to check me out, and that upon seeing me in this state, rambling on about the Fat Man he could no more see than one sees butterflies in one's stomach, he would turn and say to the doctor, "Maybe you should keep her for a few days."

I drove away, taking corner after corner as quickly as I could— without breaking the speed limit, of course. I had to lose whoever might be behind me. In less than twenty minutes, I found myself at the beachfront at a waterfront park, overlooking the incoming tide. I wept for a while and finally headed home.

I canceled my next scheduled appointment with Ms. T, deciding I was not ready to be confined to a white, lifeless hospital ward. She had been gracious on the phone, saying only, "Call me for an appointment anytime you want to talk. I'm here on Tuesdays and Thursdays."

The next weeks were riddled with encounters with the Fat Man. He lurked behind the faces of almost everyone I knew. One Wednesday, I attended the Bible study I regularly participated in and found him to be especially fat and mean that evening. The leader of our study was a gregarious, young, towheaded man who enjoyed engaging our members in lively, controversial conversations. This particular evening, the topic was marriage. You know the shtick: Wives should submit to husbands, but it's okay because husbands are supposed to love their wives. Of course, most of the six husbands in our group were outlandishly enthusiastic throughout the discussion. My own husband sat beside me quietly, no doubt knowing that if I began to speak, the tone of the discussion would shift from unchallenged zeal to tentative, polite argument. Since my prior experience with the Baptist pastor, I had edged my way into several conversations with various spiritual "leaders," inquiring and engaging debate around the issues related to a woman's place in the church and the family. I needed to believe, for the sake of my own marriage, that I was a partner—a sometimes-leading, sometimes-following, sometimes-side-by-side partner.

The Fat Man no longer threatened me by encouraging perpetual silence in the presence of other Christians. Instead, of late, he frequently took a divergent tact of reprimanding everything I said after the fact. This night was a key example of such attacks.

I entered the conversation, knowing that there would be an unseen participant. As I had expected, smiles remained pasted on faces around the circle as I said, "I'm not so sure the head of the household thing necessarily means the man is the leader and the woman the follower. What if the wife is better than the husband at, say, managing money? She makes wise investments and plays the stock market with good returns. Wouldn't it be stupid for her to give leadership of that area over to her not-so-savvy husband? Wouldn't it make very little sense to give in to his ideas about an investment if she knew his ideas were bad, just in the interest of submission?"

Around the room, one by one, eyes turned to our blond-haired leader. He had his Bible open to the "submit" verses. He reached for the Book as I heard the Fat Man's voice, more bellowing and commanding than usual: *Shut up now while you still have friends. The whole Christian world believes in wives submitting. Who are you to call God's word into question?* Believe it or not, I think I wanted to listen to him and shut my mouth, but I could not stop this discussion, as I had been unable to stop so many others before it. Some growing thing inside of me no longer had the tolerance to remain silent, and I seemed to be developing a knack for offending people. Certainly, I would only agonize over it later, in the middle of the night. I could ignore the Fat Man now, but I would pay later.

Finally, the leader spoke. He held his Bible up to us with his left hand and gestured convincingly with his right. "It would be hard for a woman to give in under those circumstances, I grant you. And a wise man would do well to listen to such a wife on financial matters. Even so, if he continued to insist on his way, she should submit. We know that God blesses those who are obedient to Him. God would take care of that wife, but only if she did what was right according to the Word. If she submitted and her husband was wrong, he would have to answer to God, but she would have done the right thing." Same argument as always. The woman gets her reward in heaven and the man gets his way on earth.

I had little control over what I did next. I took the hypothetical to the most ridiculous conclusion I could come up with. Out of the corner of my eye, I saw my husband look down slightly. He must have known where I was going, must have sensed I was about to get nasty. "And if he wants to beat her up or rape her, she should submit, too, because the first shall be last and the last will be first. Right? She'll get an extra jewel in her crown, and he'll get to beat his wife. Everybody's happy? Where do you draw the line? Does submit mean the same thing no matter the situation or only in certain circumstances? And who decides when it's appropriate? Is it possible these verses have nothing to do with one person obeying another person? Is it possible we're missing the point somehow, altogether?" *Hysterical. Let it go. You'll lose them this way. What do you think you know that your leader doesn't know? He's been to seminary. You're just a hysterical idiot.*

Everyone was silent for a moment. Finally, the leader's wife spoke up with a question of her own, "What do you think the verses mean, Cami?"

"I have no idea," I snapped. "And neither do you. Your way of thinking about them makes sense only in a perfect world. If you haven't noticed, that doesn't apply here on planet Earth."

An hour later, in the car on the way home I repeated the Fat Man's words to my husband. "What an idiot I am. I always get into arguments about this. What does it matter? It's more important to keep my friends than to make a point, right?"

To his credit, he responded quietly, "Oh, I don't know. The purpose of the study is to talk about what we think the Scriptures mean. I mean, why can't you say what you think? If they can't handle a little discussion, they shouldn't come. Anyway, I think you're right. You don't need me telling you what to do. Why does any woman need that?"

I sat for a moment in gratitude for my husband's generosity in this moment before reviling myself once again. "I know, but I made a total fool of myself arguing against everyone. Now they'll think I'm argumentative and controversial."

"You are. So what? Somebody has to be. I don't have the guts, and I'm not quick enough on my feet. I thought the conversation was boring until you spoke up. Don't worry about it."

Ah, the cry of my heart—to NOT "worry about it."

That night I stayed alert until long beyond midnight. I reviewed the Bible study. I peeled each word like fruit ripened to the point of fermentation. I chopped up my attitude and my image until I saw myself on the cutting board in tiny pieces. But at about three in the morning, when I began to despair of getting to sleep before the alarm stole the silence away from me, it occurred to me that I had heard another voice, besides that of the Fat Man, the night before. There had been a wild but whispering articulation urging me to speak my mind. I had taken notice of the Fat Man, but had I not given privilege to the Other voice, at least in the moment? I had spoken up in spite of the warnings against it. True, I ransomed my latent peace of mind for having a voice in the group. I had known *he* would take me to task when I got home, but I had chosen to speak, nonetheless.

What if the Fat Man was speaking so loudly through this night because he sensed he was losing me? Unable to keep me silent, he bellowed in my ear, commanding me to shut up. Perhaps he took me to task through the dark hours because he was hungry. I had deprived him of his nourishment—my obedience.

"I'll be damned if I don't starve you to death," I said out loud and drifted to sleep.

I called my therapist. At my next session, Ms. T sipped her iced mocha while I settled myself comfortably into her cozy office. I wanted to be still and silent for a moment or two before divulging my new secret. She waited. I waited. I thought she might recognize something new in me, something differing from the theme song I had been singing at our previous meeting. I wanted her to say, "You look different, what is it?" She said nothing, but remained expectant, like an improvisational actor, for me to make an offer.

"Oh, all right," I started. "I heard another voice last week." Would she now think I was really nuts? A second voice? Would she begin to suspect psychosis? Would she recommend lithium?

"Mm-hmm. Go on," is all she said.

"It was a feminine, raspy voice with a lot of vehemence and anger."

"I've heard her."

I nearly dropped out of my chair. "What do you mean you've heard her? I've only just heard her this week."

"I can't believe that. She's the first one I heard the day we met."

"What did she say?"

"She said, 'I've got a Fat Man on my chest.'" Ms. T sipped, looked up at me and raised an eyebrow. "Don't you remember?"

"I said that," I argued.

"So you did," she responded.

Again, I was confused. I was talking about a voice that etched out space against the nagging, the guiltifying of the Fat Man. I was telling her about a rebellion I was noticing. Another character was coming alive in my head, just now, not six months ago. I became quiet for a long time. In fact, I had almost forgotten Ms. T was in the room with me so that when she spoke, she startled me with her voice.

"Tell me some of the things she has been saying."

"Oh. It's crazy."

"Mm-hmm. Go on."

"She says, 'Say it. Speak up. So what if he doesn't like you. What's the worst that can happen? Screw trying to make the grade. You know you can do it. Do what you can. You're not perfect; get over it. Be obnoxious. Take a chance. Dream a little. Flip her off. Don't apologize. You have the right.'" I paused. So many of her words were coming forth. Suddenly I was struck by an alarming thought. "She sounds insensitive."

"Does she? To whom?"

"To other people. I've always avoided doing the things she's suggesting."

"Always?"

"No. But *usually* I've tried to avoid them."

"Because if you did the things she's suggesting, it would mean?" She sipped her straw and recrossed her legs, then leaned forward to match the position I had taken up while enumerating the things I had been hearing from this other voice.

"It would mean that I was not a nice person; that someone might become angry with me." I breathed in and held my air for a long moment. Then I began to cry. It was not the frustrated gushing of someone in the fight of her life. It was a gentle trickle, like a spring finding its way to the surface. "It would mean I couldn't control what others felt about me, and that might mean they could hurt me or reject me."

I raised my head to see if my revelation that the Fat Man had been protecting me had been as startling to Ms. T as it had been to me. Her response was more startling, still. I will never forget her words. "I'm gaining a better appreciation for your Fat Man all the time. I'd like us to talk to him directly. Could we invite him in next week?"

I tipped my head and looked at her quizzically. "I guess so," I said.

This session had moved slowly. I felt as if I were in a time tunnel filled with thick gray matter that made movement sluggish. I made an appointment for the following week and went home to take a nap.

"Okay. Let's go," she said, placing another chair beside mine. I had vague memories of my mother setting two places at the table for Lulu and Leelee, my childhood imaginary friends. I had to smile, despite the heaviness on my chest when Ms. T began interrogating me about what the Fat Man looked like.

"He's extremely obese, overflowing the chair. And he's glaring at me." I could see him in the chair she'd placed beside me and was uncomfortable with his proximity.

"May I interview him?"

"Go ahead."

"All right." She shifted her position and poised her pen above her notepad. "Mr. Fat Man, you're a very influential person in Cami's life. I appreciate you joining us today."

He spoke aloud then. It was the first time I'd ever heard him speak directly to another person. "It's the least I can do," he replied indolently.

"I agree." Ms. T's tone was so confident. It struck me that she did not seem frightened of him in the slightest. "I'd like to ask you a few questions about your relationship with Cami."

"Shoot. I'll tell you anything you want to know." He was taking a playful tone, but there was an insidiousness behind it.

"Great. Let's start with your role in Cami's life. What do you see as your job with her?"

"Well, of course, I do a number of things, but my primary job is to make sure she plays by the rules. I remind her of the consequences of various behaviors. I do my best to catch her before she blows it, but she's impulsive, so sometimes I have to discuss an incident with her after the fact."

Ms. T leaned toward him. "So how do you go about making her play be the rules? What does that mean?"

"I speak to her. I tell her to shut up when she is talking too much. Sometimes she refuses to listen. When this happens, I give her hell later."

"Why do you do that? What's in it for you?"

Indignantly the Fat Man replied, "There's nothing in it for me. I do it selflessly. I do it to keep her tightly within a safe set of boundaries she can clearly understand. I do it to teach her a lesson, to keep her from undertaking the same stupid course of action on some other occasion. I do it all to protect her."

"Oh really?" Ms. T said calmly. "But is all of this effort necessary? I don't believe she needs you to tell her how to think about her behavior. Doesn't she know that on her own?"

"Well, you wouldn't know it to watch her. She has a lot of opinions, you know. I'm the only one who can shut her up."

I listened in silence to his perspective, reserving any reflection for later.

"I don't get it. Why does she need to shut up? Don't other people like what she has to say?"

"Sometimes," he conceded. "Some people have commented to her that they appreciate what she says, even when it is controversial. That just encourages her."

"What do you have against her being encouraged?" Ms. T leaned back again and folded her arms.

"Don't assume I hate her, Ms. T. She's very important to me. I do all of this for her own benefit." His voice grew softer. "I didn't always have to be so tough, you know. She used to listen more readily. But I'm growing tired of being ignored and unappreciated. You know, she owes a lot to me. If it hadn't been for me, she wouldn't have made it through her childhood."

"How do you mean?"

"Well, I directed her through her parents' fighting and through the obstacle course of her mother's second marriage. If it hadn't been for me, she wouldn't have known how to get out of the way of her stepfather. Or when to step in and stop the flow of an argument. Or how to protect her brothers."

"Mr. Fat Man, again, I'm confused. I can understand you wanting to step in and protect a child, but you've gotten mean in recent years. The way I understand it, you threaten and cajole her into strict conformity to something you sickly say is for her own good. But clearly—I mean, she has chest pains—your efforts aren't doing her good at this point. What's this all really about?"

"Well, she still needs my input, but she's less inclined to listen than she used to be."

"Although I'm grateful you've kept her safe, I disagree that she still needs your strategies. I think she's a big girl now, and she doesn't need your criticism anymore. In fact, I'm sick of it. I'm sick of the way you treat her. According to my calculation, it's time you stop this nastiness." Ms. T was looking at him intently. She had clearly decided the Fat Man had seen the last of his reign. "You and Cami need to have a talk and come up with a different arrangement. She's shown herself to be someone who can conclude for herself when to follow various sets of rules. You're causing her a lot of grief, and I'm at a loss as to understand why."

"She needs me."

"I don't believe it. What does she need you for, specifically?"

The Fat Man took a breath and started his list. "She needs me to remind her to drive the speed limit, to work out three times a week, to eat properly, to be kind to strangers, to remember Mother's Day, to get people to like her, to be a good wife, to . . ."

Ms. T cut him off. "Mr. Fat Man, excuse me, but even the little I know of Cami, I know she is alert and intelligent. I simply cannot buy what you are saying. I think she can absolutely do all of those things on her own, the way she wants to do them. It's time for a change, I'm afraid. You've outlived your usefulness. You're going to have to give her up."

I was surprised to see him yield. Deflated from his usual cocky self, he seemed almost willing to concede defeat.

"You see," Ms. T began, "I think Cami gets what you are about. She knows your ploys and she is tired of them. Don't get me wrong, she appreciates the protection you gave her when she was small, but that's over now. Don't you think she can see how little she needs you at this point?"

"Yes. I suppose I do." He deflated further. I was dumbstruck. He looked smaller than he had in many years.

"And you must be tired, too. This has been a very long marathon for you."

He nodded. "I am very tired. I used to like my role, but you're right, she doesn't need me. I'd like a divorce, not with equal division of property even, but with my dignity. I'd like to go find another relationship where my skills can be utilized better."

"Indeed," Ms. T said. "Well, Mr. Fat Man, I think you've had your say. I'd like to give Cami an opportunity to reflect on what you have shared and help her parse out what she might be willing to do about this relationship the two of you have. So, I thank you for coming and talking with me. Do you have any last words before we ask you to leave?"

He was silent for a moment. "One thing." Another pause. "There's been talk of killing me. I'd like you to tell her that she doesn't have to do that. I can move on. Tell her that I don't want to die. What I do is important, even if it's not for her anymore."

I had never seen him humble before. Was I mistaken or was he begging? I had never known him to be so willing to compromise. He departed, for the time being, considerably thinner and with slumping shoulders.

I took his former seat and cried silently for a few minutes before leaving, myself.

I did, indeed, put in a great deal of reflection as to how to proceed after hearing the Fat Man verbalize his motivations and intentions. Some may not think I made the wisest decision, when you hear what I did. It may be that when you face off with your own Fat Man, you will bring your story to some variant conclusion. But for me, my decision was adequate—not perfect, but adequate. I sat at my computer and prepared a certificate of divorce for the two of us to sign and a restraining order. You see, I knew that his plea that I not kill him was more than merely his own fear of dying. He was, quite simply, unkillable. I knew I would hear echoes of him in various places. At school, in my parents' homes, during job interviews, he would be resurrected. Sometimes, I suspected, I would feel inclined to invite him. I needed something that would give me leverage to push him away. To remind him he was free to go. It was imperative that I devise a way to help myself remember I had the right NOT to listen to his attempts at luring me to return to him. You see, I knew him well, and I could imagine him watching me from a distance, gesturing at me, hollering for my attention, and I was certain that it would take a while before I was confident enough to cut him loose completely.

The restraining order required him to remain one hundred yards away from my person and property. The divorce certificate was not fancy. It read as follows:

Certificate of Divorce

This document certifies that the parties named below have legally dissolved their partnership and are hereby divorced as of the date: 29 March, 2000.

All property belonging to first said party shall be returned to her upon the injunction of this dissolution. Second said party shall not be granted property in any amount.

Sincere thanks for early services are hereby extended to the second party. All matrimonial agreements are henceforth and permanently canceled.

First Party: ________________

Second Party: ________________

After I had prepared all the documents, I made an appointment to meet him for a final meal at a local restaurant, a neutral place, and made a reservation for two. I imagine the waiter believed I was completely out of my mind when I insisted he place a plate of food in front of the seemingly empty chair across from me, but I didn't care. I imagine he may have called the manager into the wait-station to observe me as I began speaking, aloud, to my apparently invisible dinner partner. And I imagine he might have considered calling the police when he tried to interrupt to me to ask if I wanted dessert, and I responded with, "No thank you. And can you please leave us alone. We are in the middle of an important conversation."

I told the Fat Man that he had been invaluable in the early years and that I appreciated the way he had kept me safe, but that the time had come for us to part. I told him that I had grown beyond him. I wanted my independence and to see if I could make it on my own. I had been indebted to him for far too long. Now he could go. He got cold feet and tried to reason with me, of course, and to bully me back into compliance by saying that divorce was strictly forbidden by any Christian standard, but I was primed for his reticence to leave and had my defense ready. I simply held up my hand to stop his voice and remarked that if I opted to disregard his rules, or any rules, for that matter, it was my choice to make. Then I handed him the restraining order and the divorce decree and required him to sign both.

I paid our bill and left him sitting at the table alone. The air outside was nippy and dry. After getting into my car, I glanced back and saw the Fat Man coming out of the restaurant, looking for me, but I was not afraid of him, now. I drove away confidently.

I have seen him at a distance from time to time since then. Once, I saw him lurking outside the window of a class I was teaching. He didn't dare come inside, but he stood, looking in, shaking his head at me disapprovingly. My students must have been baffled when I stopped my lecture, dug into my briefcase and pulled out the documents I always carry with me. They watched me with perplexed gazes as I walked to the window and taped the restraining order onto the glass, facing outward for him to see. I didn't care what they thought; measures had to be taken to remind the Fat Man that he had no claim on me anymore.

Other times, I have had only reach into my pocket and touch the restraining order or pull out the divorce decree and re-read it, and I have been reminded that I have the right not to take notice of him. One wonders, perhaps, if I will ever be entirely free of his presence. I doubt it, but I am no longer afraid of him.

The other day, I wandered through a park near my home on a peaceful afternoon. The autumn atmosphere, with its turning leaves and earthy aromas, made me full of joy to be alive. I observed the other patrons, wondering if they were basking in the environs as much as I was. A young woman, perhaps fourteen years of age, caught my eye. She was stationed on a bench inside one of the many gazebos, and she was crying, inaudibly. My first instinct was to go to her and ask if I could be of assistance. I started in her direction but halted when I saw who was beside her at the picnic table. The Fat Man was leaning into her, speaking quietly but sneeringly. He glanced up and caught my eye. I turned on my heel, walked away, returned to the trail, and continued my lazy promenade. I considered how that young woman had a long, laborious journey in front of her. She was in good but brutal hands. I wished her well.

THE SWORD-BEARER

NOTE: The character in this story came to me, as you will read, when I visited Italy the summer after graduating from my master's program. There was something in the giant, old, ominous, severe building that made me burn with regret for all of the seriousness I'd carried in my life since I was a little girl—especially after, when I was about fourteen years old, I'd joined a very fundamentalist religious sect, myself. The image of the little sword-bearing creature I describe in the scenes below came to me just as I tell. But working with this part to find out what she really needed in order to be relieved of her burden took many years. During those years, I often went back to the church in my mind's eye and spent time with her, trying to coax her to tell me what would help her unburden herself. Here I represent the story as if it happened in a few minutes, but the fact is, it was a great effort to convince this part of myself that she could trust the grown-up version of me to help her.

Reader, be patient with exiled parts. They are often very frightened and won't want to come out of hiding until they know they will be safe.

Rome was hot and overtaken with tourists that summer. The concrete inside the walls of the Vatican City radiated in waves from the sun, and I was grateful as we approached the narthex, where stone floors and the marble interior would give us reprieve, even if the body heat from the hordes of travelers and devotees pressed into the shelter right along with us.

Having read about the significant art inside the basilica we were entering, but not being overly familiar with the trappings of Catholic devotion, I didn't know to expect supplicants to be crawling—hands folded in prayer—into the cathedral, including the tiny woman shuffling through the entryway on her knees in front of me. She bent and kissed the dirty floor every few feet until she reached the Door of the Sacraments. I stood aside to give her space to enter, holding back the line of people desperate to enter the cathedral on this acrid day. Much as I wanted to get inside, myself, I felt this devoted woman deserved to enter without being trampled. As soon as she was safely inside the domed structure, I crossed the threshold myself and stood to the right, waiting for the rest of my group of four who'd been gobbled up in the masses somewhere several yards behind me.

Michelangelo's *Pietà* was not far into the nave, so as soon as my husband and our two friends joined me, we sauntered over to look at the famous marble sculpture through the bullet proof glass that protected it from the public. Mary, holding her beloved son, just taken down from the cross, bore a resigned expression—mirroring how I myself felt after years of following Jesus and trying to keep the overly rigid rules of the particular brand of Evangelicalism I'd espoused when I was only fourteen—when my family was falling apart and my mother was remarrying, bringing a stranger into our house. When I needed consistency and guidance and a place to go that wasn't home. When I didn't know that misogyny was at the heart of all I was signing up for. But now . . . *ah* . . . twenty years hence, the efforts of being a good, submissive Christian woman, of carefully curating every thought, word, and deed to make sure I didn't upset God, had made me so tired in the long run. I was here in Rome for a post-graduation trip after getting my master's degree, but I was also here as a weary devotee to Jesus, grown exhausted from trying to jump through mental hoops to not only please a God who required blood sacrifice and feminine submission, but also for his followers believe in the magic of such improbable things as multiplied fishes and loaves, people coming back from the dead, and perfect marriages based on a hierarchy I didn't really buy in to.

Mary and I have a lot in common, I thought, while the others talked about the centuries of art closing in on us from every direction. We'd brought along a book that would guide us through the masterpieces here, giving us the history of the artists and each of their grand works. I wanted to follow the self-guided tour along with the others, but I was so taken by Mary's expression that I lingered overly long at the *Pietà* as the group moved counter-clockwise to the next chapel.

Mary was only a teenager when Jesus had come into her life, too. She'd been devoted to him—as I had—following and praying and hoping, until tragedy led to the moment of defeat depicted in the sculpture: Jesus, beaten, hung on a tree, and taken down dead, crumpled into nothing but a limp pile of bones and bloodied flesh, cradled now by the woman who had traveled to Bethlehem to give birth to him, the child she had conceived through a horrible miracle some thirty-three years earlier. And although my experience was of a totally different and less dramatic nature, I was certainly at a moment of defeat in my own life now, too, and feeling Jesus to be ineffectual and limp. And as with the moment Mary held her son in her arms after his death, I didn't know if there would be a resurrection for me. I was desperate to leave the marriage I'd started in my youth—too early to know I would one day wish for independence, too young to know a woman in her mid-thirties will not be the same wide-eyed innocent girl she was when she was twenty and clung to the idea of miracles.

The smell of incense and the cool air of the dark cavern hit my senses. When I finally turned away from Mary and her burden, my eyes took some time to adjust before I could apprehend the rest of the basilica. There was the statue of St. Peter, with his foot rubbed raw from pilgrims touching him in supplication. And there was the massive altar made of gold and bronze. And there were the gold flecks in the mosaics sparkling from the dome, accusing the church of greed and gluttony.

I took in the scope with a feeling of awe—and to be honest, some general judgement of religion, rapidly lapsing Evangelical Christian that I was. Not lapsed, you see, but still lapsing. I was on my way out, but I wasn't gone yet. My faith was fading, but very slowly, mind you. Grad school had challenged me, taught me to think of my own inner reality as something to be questioned, of "God" as a construct instead of a solid truth. I was a therapist now, advocating for my clients to step outside their stuck stories to think—and by virtue of thinking, to feel—differently. To heal. I took my work and my calling as a healer very seriously, but of course, I was a wounded healer, for what healer is not wounded? That is how we know people need healing; we've been hurt, ourselves.

But all of this—my fading faith, my disillusionment with my marriage, my close contact with people in terrible crisis—was new. And heavy. I could see the loss of someone I'd known myself to be on the horizon, and I wasn't sure how I would shoulder that loss.

I glanced around without success for my group—my husband and the two friends we were backpacking though Europe with. But they'd been consumed again by the crowd. The pews in the main sanctuary were peppered with true worshippers, and I considered joining them to try to connect to something numinous—to try and *feel* into the God who had inspired a faith so fervent it threw gold and art and incense at Him to please Him. The houses of worship I'd frequented over the past two decades had been plain spaces, unadorned with the gaudiness present here in St. Peter's.

Strangely, I found that the deeper into the sanctuary I ventured, the more I did feel the presence of *something*. I felt the sweltering summer day outside become a distant thought. And I felt the marriage that was holding on by a thread, the devotion to a Savior who'd had to die to keep me out of eternal damnation, the identity as a good Christian girl I'd been desperately clinging to—all of it—drift out of my consciousness. I let my judgments go and allowed the sense of mystery encrusted in the history of the place to envelop me. In the chapel of St. Sebastian, patron of soldiers and athletes, I found a seat and let myself become mesmerized by the candles lit in supplication that burned in front of the mosaic of Sebastian's tortured body.

Tied to a tree and riddled with arrows, Sebastian looked to me more befuddled than frightened, and as I studied the image of the angels above him and the crowd surrounding him, I wondered if he suspected he would live through this first execution and have to face another one—death by clubbing—when he would survive his first torture. Did he know he would be nursed back to health, only to have to do the whole martyr thing all over again? I shuddered to think of being killed for one's faith not once but twice—

of my faithfulness being put to such a test, over and over. I would surely fail the first test and never make it to the second.

I allowed a few tears as I considered my failed devotion.

Suddenly, out of the corner of my eye, I saw a fluttering movement. I looked closely in the shadows of the chapel, and there I saw her. A tiny girl. She was wearing a tattered blue dress, ripped at the hemline. Her dirty, bare feet were bloodied—probably from walking on the concrete and stones in the Holy City, for how long I couldn't know. She was leaning against the wall just inside the arch, shoulders folding in toward her chest. Her long, straight, dishwater blond hair hung in her face. She couldn't have been older than eight years old.

I observed her carefully. In her hands she held up, with some effort, a gigantic sword, worthy of Arthur's knights. It was nearly as long as she was tall, with a sparkling silver double-edged blade, clearly too heavy for her small frame, and she strained under the weight of it. The look in her eyes, which she flitted hitherto and fro, decried the stress of wandering barefoot through the world carrying the terrible burden of that sword.

Though she was clearly in distress and hovering in the shadows as if hiding from something or someone, she met my eyes the moment they were turned on her with concern. I raised my eyebrows at her and cocked my head, my own blond ponytail swinging away from the dried sweat on my neck with the motion. Her expression was pleading.

I squinted at St. Sebastian and knew why she hid in his chapel in particular. She was a warrior, this Sword-Bearer, though what she was fighting against I didn't know.

Compassion flooded me, and I whispered to her, "Child, come sit for a moment, you look exhausted."

She shook her head vigorously. "Can't," was all she uttered. Her voice was raspy, as if she'd shouted it away at a football game the day before.

Her resistance to coming to the pew for a rest invoked a terrible sadness inside me, and I could feel that sadness matched by hers—as if she wanted nothing more in all the world than to sit for a time. But for some reason, she could not.

I rose, scooted sideways out my pew, and slowly approached her.

With her soiled and bruised feet, she tried to back away from me, pressing herself fully against the wall that already held her upright, and hoisted her sword an inch or two higher, wielding it in my direction, as if I certainly meant her harm. But in her eyes I could see she very much wished to avoid a fight with me. As I got closer, I could see that her arms were wiry—strong from carrying this too-heavy weapon for God-knew-how-long, but also thin. She was malnourished. Her clavicle protruded through the tatters of her dirty dress. And she stank—of sweat and dirt and tears and exhaustion.

When I was close enough for her to swipe me with her sword, I knelt on the stone floor and looked at her, face-to-face. "What's your name, little one?" I whispered the words.

She studied me; her blue eyes fixed on me with apprehension. "I can't tell you," she said.

"Well, if you can't tell me your name, can you put down your sword and give your arms a rest?" I offered. "I won't hurt you."

"Can't," she said once again.

I looked around at the few other tourists who had seated themselves in the chapel, wanting to appeal to someone more experienced with children to help me calm this distressed young one, but no one paid either of us any mind.

I could have walked away and left her to the clergy to deal with, but by this time in my relationship with any church I didn't have so much trust in clergy to do the right thing. So, I tried again.

"That looks like a pretty heavy burden you're carrying, little Sword-Bearer," I said, studying the weapon from up close now. "What sort of danger are you fighting against?"

To my surprise, her face relaxed and she looked me in the eye as if I'd got onto the right line of questioning at last. "Just anything," she breathed.

"Just anything?" I echoed. "Well, it's a pretty big sword for just anything. Why do you have to keep such vigilance?"

Now, I saw that my curiosity softened her. She lowered the blade of her sword to the floor of the chapel with a metallic clunk that echoed through the whole basilica, though she held onto the grip, and let a tear slip down her cheek. "I simply must," is all she said, shaking her head with obvious despair.

"Do you never relax?" I asked.

She shook her head. "Never."

I nodded in understanding. I'd certainly wended my way through my own childhood without a moment's rest as well. In fact, though I hadn't carried a literal sword, I'd been on alert and had abandoned my innocence so early I couldn't recall what it felt like to be a child at all. I saw the same loss in this small one standing before me.

"What happened?" I thought I would try again to see if she would open her story to me.

"I lost it so long ago, I don't really remember," she said. By now she'd relaxed her hold on the hilt of her sword and leaned against the weapon as if it were a cane keeping her upright. She tipped her head back and looked up beyond our chapel toward St. Peter's central dome.

"What did you lose?" I pressed, by now so curious about this little waif that I felt I simply had to help her if I could.

My husband and our friends were gone to the Sistine Chapel point, I supposed. But I was so rapt by the Sword-Bearer and the grief in her eyes that I nearly forgot that I was in Italy, in Vatican City, far away from home, speaking to an obviously homeless child in St. Sebastian's chapel. I was only aware of the circle between the two of us, our locked gazes.

"What did you lose?" I asked again.

"Happiness." She spoke so quietly I wasn't sure I heard.

"Happiness?" I wanted to be sure.

"Well, more like glee, really," she clarified.

At the word "glee" I felt my own spirit break. I didn't know what "glee" felt like in the body either. To my recollection, it wasn't a word I'd ever even used.

Our eyes were looking into one another now, some other-worldly transmission happening between us. My pity for her grew with every breath we took, and tears streamed freely down my face. In fact, I could feel our inhales and aspirations coordinating, heaving in and out in tandem. I had the strongest urge to wrap my arms around her and squeeze her grip on that sword loose so that she could be free of it, but I worried I would startle her into action rather than relieve her of her burden.

"What can be done for you?" I asked her. The question was as much for me as it was for her. What could be done with the burden of my own childhood pain, and now the tragic and sometimes brutal stories of my clients? And of course, what could be done with the marriage I didn't want but couldn't escape without committing sin? And the doctrines of my church? To believe the implausible, to perform with perfection, to know you are never good enough, to bear the guilt of a Man's death exchanged for your life. To always worry you would go to hell if so much as a *belief* was amiss. I felt as weary as she looked. What could be done? I'd weighed every option, sliced every possibility open with my own sharp sword, and could find no answer. Leave Jesus? Divorce my husband? Go rogue? Unthinkable unless I was willing to leave my whole community of friends behind—including these two friends who at this very moment were cavorting with my husband under Michelangelo's frescos, reveling in representations of God as a bearded man, a man who created men, giving men dominion over all creatures, including women.

"What can be done? To relieve this burden?" I repeated.

She shook her head. She didn't know. But by now she would let me lead her to a pew at the back of the chapel. She dragged her sword on the floor behind her. The sound of its scraping against the stone was so irritating that I was shocked the priest leading mass at the pulpit did not pause to ask us to leave. But no one turned so much as a scowl in our direction.

The little Sword-Bearer allowed me to take her by the hand and to sit her beside me. She let me put my palm on the back of her dirty head and stroke her hair. We both let our tears flow until they were spent. And then she allowed me to gently prod her into a reclining position where I held her in my arms like Jesus being cradled by Mary in the *Pietà* across the basilica. She lay her head against the crook of my arm and let her sword rest, unclutched, but nestled in the crook of her own arm.

We stayed that way for a very long time. I don't know how long. An hour? Three hours? No one came for me. Maybe they looked, but I never found out.

Then, at some point, I wondered what to do with this child I was holding. I wanted our sacred and mutual understanding to go on forever, but I couldn't abandon those I'd come with and sneak away with a homeless sword-bearing urchin, could I?

Just as I was puzzling over what to do next, she spoke. "Roller skates," she murmured.

"What?" I asked.

"You asked me what could be done for me," she reminded me, "you know, to help me."

"Oh, yes," I said.

"Roller skates," she repeated. "I've always wanted roller skates."

"Oh, yes," I said again. What a thing! I hadn't expected such a concrete answer when I'd asked the question. And yet, I understood her. I'd always wanted my own pair of roller skates, too—wanted to have had the freedom to sail on the street outside my childhood house past the trees and neighbors, wanted to have been able to roll away faster than anyone could catch me from the fighting and anger in my home. But we'd been too poor and my parents too inattentive for me to have ever gotten those skates. I pondered her request, yearning more than anything to get this child what she asked for. "I wonder if we can find any in Rome?"

"Probably not." The hopelessness in her voice woke something inside me.

Rebellion. Determination.

We sat with silence between us again for a few moments as the priest read the liturgy and the parishioners provided responses to his calls.

Peace be with you.

And also with you.

I made a decision. "Well, let's find out."

I nudged her to indicate we should stand, and she rose with enthusiasm. Not glee, perhaps, but something akin to hope. I held out my hand to take the sword from her. She reluctantly handed it over, and I could see her heave a deep exhale with the absence of its encumbrance. It was heavier than I had imagined, but surely not as heavy for me as it was for her. Together we exited through the crowds, past St. Peter's statue . . . saluting the *Pietà* once again . . . through the Door of Sacraments . . . out of the narthex . . . onto the Piazza San Pedro . . . and then out of Vatican City altogether. To fulfill a new sacrament—a personal one. To find a pair of roller skates for each of us.

ODE TO THE
WELL-WOMAN'S CATALYST

NOTE: A word about the conventions in the story you are about to read: You will notice that I refer to the people with whom I'd developed "codependent" relationships without using possessive pronouns. In other words, "my" mother is referred to as "the" mother and "my" husband is referred to as "the" husband.

I wrote this story, as I mentioned in the introduction, after I had an experience with a man who startled me by looking at me differently than anyone had ever looked at me. That relationship was to be short-lived but was to serve as a catalyst to an awakening—to a realization that I often felt like little more than a blank screen for other people's projections. This wonderful man who looked at me so deeply served as an anchor for me as I learned to listen to the voice of my inner champion: the Well-Woman.

So, while the language in the story is cryptic at times, I wrote this it as it came to me and with a commitment to be true to the Well-Woman's voice, however it showed up. As you read it, you may be bumped in the beginning by the depersonalization of some of the other characters, but by the end, I think you'll understand why I wrote it that way.

You'll also see that TIME is obfuscated in the story whenever the narration returns to encounters with this man, the Well-Woman's catalyst (Adam). It may help you to know I wrote the entire story with my eyes closed as if in a lucid dream. The Well-Woman arrived as a character who was timeless and timely and present with me for about three months every time I sat at my computer, put my fingers on the key-board, and closed my lids. She showed me what to write and I obeyed her.

I was thirty-four years old when I wrote the Well-Woman —a couple of years after identifying the Fat Man energy and beginning to attend to the Sword-Bearer's bur-dens/wounds (about a year after the trip to the Vatican City described in the that second story, in fact). So she came to my consciousness during the same period of time as the other two, but my relationship with her has evolved and flourished. To this day, I do a daily Well-Woman meditation and keep a journal of what I hear that voice inside me saying. This inner champion is the voice I turn to for advice about everything from business to love to health—everything.

May you find and listen to the voice of your own Inner Champion, reader

I was, quite possibly, conceived in the back seat of a car. The young teenagers in question might have been hurried, excited, and clandestine in their preparations for the event. They were, no doubt, frightened of being found out; both of my grandmothers were formidable forces in their own very different ways, and I have heard stories of each of them ardently warning their adoles-cent children against the possible perils of sex and pregnancy. Nevertheless, on some September afternoon (I count backward from my birthdate to determine this), the kids cut sixth period, and the red Ford made its way into a field with tall grass or, per-haps, into a forested area just beyond the city limits.

In an equally haphazard way, I spent my first few years in a small trailer house at the edge of a little town called BrierRose. The lot was shoddy; rubble and old cars littered the yard. It was the kind of place middle class people sneer at and criticize when forced to drive through less fortunate neighborhoods. Thankfully, I had never heard the term "trailer trash" while I lived in this tiny, yellowing home. It seemed a happy place to me with my two dogs and a flamboyant neighbor I called "Aunt Clara."

In the yard, there was a well. Time and again, the young mother warned me against getting too close to it, but I was only three years old. Exploring was my raison d'être. Fortunately, Aunt Clara was of a mind that if a child gets the opportunity to experience the world on her own terms, she will be less likely to sneak around and get hurt. Often, when the mother was taking care of the new baby brother—who was born when I was two—or doing the grocery shopping, Aunt Clara would take me to look into the well.

"Look deep down in," she would say, "you can see the future if you strain."

I strained and strained, but all I could see on a sunny day was my reflection next to wild Aunt Clara's.

Eventually, the new baby started to toddle around and we began to feel cramped in our little dwelling. We moved to a slightly larger place on the property of relative—a real aunt—and I never saw my well or my Aunt Clara again. At the new house, a place we forever refer to as the "green house," (yes, because it was painted green) my parents' marriage began to sour. It is possible it had never really accrued much substance, but these are the days I remember as the beginning of the violence. I ducked and avoided the dishes that were heaved through the air. I took on the care of the baby brother, the first of a total of three who would need to be cared for in the coming years during these feuds, and I learned how not to make people angry.

More than thirty years later I have perfected the art of keeping people happy and safe. I never rebelled during my teenage years, nor did I break any of the commandments I learned about in church. Eventually, I married a man who needed someone to help him be happy and safe, as well. Family members have expected me to watch my tongue, or at least never to go too far when I express an opinion. I have worked as hard as possible to be kind and reliable and wise and disciplined and hospitable and warm and good. Until one day . . .

There is a swelling in my throat and constriction in my chest. It is neither the usual constriction of guilt, nor the tightening that happens as a warning that I am in danger of breaking a "sacred" rule. Rather, it is she, the Well-Woman, breast-stroking upward for air.

The night is cool, but not cold, and the sound of the ocean waves would be deafening if we were any closer to the shore.

I have heard the gurgling and gasping of her wildish nature before, but tonight she is alarmingly loud, splashing. You, Adam, lie down in the sand and I follow. Elbow to elbow we talk. You let me in further than ever before in these two years we've been friends. She strokes and kicks, up and up.

As if the roped walls surrounding the top of the well are being unraveled, one gnarled twist at a time, I feel the yanking and uncrusting of the pieces of my life. I lie in bed, saying to myself, "My composure is coming apart, and this time I don't have the power to stop it." Family members have always relied on my stability, trusting me to have an answer, an adequate response to all their woes and dilemmas. I, in my turn, having always felt like a stranger to those closest to me, have sought my place of belonging in being the healer, the answerer.

But all at once, I have begun to lose my power to heal others. I have almost lost the ability to look into the eyes of the mother, the brother, the husband sitting before me and to perceive what it is she or he is asking and to be willing to give it. In the past I have perceived and given abundantly, simply because my generosity was wanted (although it was never asked for directly, only through yearning looks or desperate voices). I can still see dimly, however, and I see in the husband's eyes that he does not like the music-listening, dancing, writing, friend-needing self I am becoming. He does not like that I am not available to him in the same way as I have been available for the past decade. He knows I am unraveling and has counted on my being raveled for too many years.

His eyes and voice plead with me for something. "You are so into yourself lately. We don't make love. You aren't into *us*. I am lonely."

Yes. I hear you. I see your pain. And it is very difficult for me to be still, I think. But I also feel the usual lie descending upon me. I am being required to sit beside him and to put my arms around his frail soul and to speak the words that promise my new trajectory is only a phase. He may want me to say, "I am struggling, but everything will be all right. I will never leave you. You are safe with me. I am as strong as ever to keep you well. What you and I have means too much for me to risk identifying with, embracing, releasing the Well-Woman who scrapes at the walls of my esophagus." But what shall I do about the progress she is making with her abrasive clawing?

What I decide to do is stand motionless. I say that it hurts me to see him hurt and, silently, I earnestly hope he has some resources of which I know nothing. May he have a friend somewhere that he has never told me about. May he have a spirituality I have not seen. May there be some strength inside of him that has nothing to do with me.

On the beach I am perfectly still. The rain comes, but I don't mind it landing on my face, my hands, my exposed ankles. I am wet. You are responding to me. I can sense your arousal, but I ignore the possibilities emerging between us until the Well-Woman's pushing, pushing, throbbing, throbbing is almost more than I can contain. I will have to roll over onto my stomach, as you did nearly an hour before. The pressure of the sand against my breasts is a relief. If I can pretend that what is happening between us is an illusion, Adam, maybe I can seize her and press her back into her darkness. That has worked for me before.

As we speak, you are hearing me in a way I am rarely heard. You seem to see a part of me I usually hide from you. I, in turn, am seeing your fear and your excitement at being near me. You, usually so guarded and on stage, drop your walls, and when you do, I see a fragility I am not expecting. It moves me.

Not a month after moving into my newly purchased house, I have what can only be described as a "getting loose from the house" dream. I dream that my cat, Charley, escapes from the house and finds her way to the edge of the freeway. I run after her, frantic for her safety and scoop her up by the scruff of the neck, struggling with her, moving into the grass along the freeway's edge and further away from the danger of the cars. She, in her turn, is determined to become free of me. And when she does, she drops into the grass and becomes a snake, one of the small garter snakes that used to inhabit the mother's strawberry garden when I was a little girl. I bend down, gather her coiled body into my cupped palms and hold tight, rushing her home.

At first, I can feel her moving inside my hands, but shortly, she settles down. When I finally reach the house and open my grip to check on her, she is shriveled and dry. Naturally, I place her with some leaves in a jar of water to rehydrate her. I watch her carefully, but after only a few moments I understand she is dead and lifeless.

This dream warns me of something, nudges me into considering what will become of me if I squeeze out the part of myself that seeks freedom and insist instead that she stay safe and silent. I speak of the dream to several people, including the husband, but the understanding of its message comes when I reread one of my favorite poems by T.S. Eliot. The line reading, "I have measured out my life with coffee spoons" strikes me hard. I have kept my wildness and creativity, my sexuality and passion locked safely in a sterile house—away from danger.

And so, the Well-Woman is near the surface, dear Adam. The next week, I see you, clasp your hand in passing in the hallway, and I begin to realize the depths from which she has come. The water in the well may be fathomless, darker than anyone can guess. I wonder if I can yet drown her by holding her under, but somehow, I know she can live through anything. I have already ignored, starved, berated, and suffocated her. I have let her enemies (Untruth, Pretending, Denial) into her waters, sent to pillage her environs and shackle her to the bottom. Still, she lives. She is not like the snake in my dream. She continues to struggle for truth.

Each day you and I meet after work in the parking lot and talk of dreams and God and poetry. An ignored and subordinated sense of each other is emerging. In your gaze, I begin to see myself differently. And I dare to think of you in a new light. I do not recognize the woman I am becoming, and yet there is something faintly familiar about her.

As I walk through my life, supposing I look the same to family and people at work, I become concerned by the certain knowledge that she will draw breath soon. The colors of my world change. Dullness mutates, inexplicably, into vibrancy all around me. Savagely, on her journey to the surface, the Well-Woman has devoured her enemies and the Pretenders are nowhere to be found. I have little strength for lies. Each thought I think comes to my lips. "My god," I lament, "where have the screens gone?" Familiar haze-making fear and worry are disappearing and all that I am seems completely exposed. What anger, disappointment, joy and lust, which had once been tolerable in taupe and mauve are brilliant and primary, screaming with vibrations. I find myself shading my eyes at the clarity of each experience. I say "I love you" or "fuck off" when it comes to me. My body pulses or is repulsed spontaneously; it demands I respond.

The husband looks at me with strange, vacant eyes. I find I absolutely cannot perceive what he is thinking now. He will have to tell me if he wants me to know, and I realize he may not have the capacity to do so. What will it mean if I can no longer play my role?

And the guilt I once lauded as a helpmate is, still, continuously absent. I dance freely. I want to write every day. I play music loudly. I enjoy the friendships of people I have avoided in the past for moral or religious reasons.

But I find that I can no longer eat. One, two, eleven pounds drop away from me. They drop even faster after the day the Well-Woman takes her first full breath. The effort of keeping her just beneath the surface has worn me down. In a brief but irrevocable moment, like the snapping of a branch from a tree, I realize that I must dare, now, to eat the fruit life offers me. Within less than once second, a commitment to myself and my truth emerges. Breathe . . . breathe . . .

Sitting alone in an empty house, I close my eyes and go deep inside to a sacred place, crossing an imagined yard, ducking under trees and coming to the edge of the hidden well. It is an old well— older than my thirty-four years. I examine the outside wall. It is perhaps six feet in diameter and made of uneven rocks cemented together with common mortar. Along the top, there is a rope, as thick as my ankle, wound around the sharp edges, and placed here, I suppose, so that one would not get cut on the rockery if reaching over into the well to draw water.

The rope is also ancient. It is browning and brittle and has been picked at by birds or people or weather so that it is no longer applied evenly all the way around the circumference of the wall. There is a wooden lid, which had once kept toxins and unwelcome objects out of the water, lying discarded and rotting on the ground a few feet away.

Reluctant to look in at first, I circle the well and then circle it again. There are odd symbols scratched into some of the rocks. I kneel and look closely to see if there is sense to be made of them. They are initials that I intuit should be familiar to me, but I cannot make a connection that clears up the mystery. Finally, I stand again and lean over the wall and look down into the center of the structure.

The water is perhaps three feet below the top of the wall. It appears absolutely bemired and black, not clean as I usually think of well-water. The scent of mildew, that dankness of places long neglected, assaults me. My eyes adjust to the dim light, and I bend in further, getting as close to the stale air as I feel I can hazard.

Suddenly, she is there. I see the crown of her head pushing through the surface of the water. Her skull caps the dark space of the narrow canal. Her face, glowing and translucent, follows. She is birthing herself, a little too quickly for my taste, into my consciousness and my world.

God, she is ugly, I think. Her long, tangled hair and pasty complexion alarm me. What have I let out of hell? Her breath smells of mud and her eyes are ravenous and jutting, seeing everything, registering her surroundings quickly. Her neck is long and slim but scratched and dirty, the residue of algae clinging to her skin there. I stand at the edge of the well wall and look down at her. Oddly enough, although she frightens me, she intrigues me, too. The shape of her face is squared off, chiseled, making me think of the Stoics. The color of her lips is the primary red of my own menstrual blood, bright in the center, darker around the edges.

When she settles her feral eyes on me, they turn tender. I am not expecting the compassion they convey and, taken by surprise at the appearance of her deep kindness toward me, I lean in and offer her my hand. It is not until her upper torso is elevated above the water line that I realize there may be unexpected and undesirable ramifications to what I am doing, and I shake her loose to run toward the house. I look back at her once. Those red lips are moving. She wishes to speak to me.

I am not ready yet to listen. She is breathing and that is enough. I open my eyes.

I make an appointment with my therapist. Realizing I cannot go this road alone and fearing that the Well-Woman may be too extraordinary for most of the people in my life to look at, I know I shall need help to hear her and follow her instructions. I find the courage to make the call when I mention her to you. I say, "I don't know what I will find down there." You say, "It is beautiful. I'm sure of that." My first impression of her is not one of beauty, but I choose to believe you because you have nothing to gain by lying to me about what you see. Adam, I know when you say I am good or beautiful, you do not mean, "Please be good and beautiful so I can be okay." You mean that you see goodness and beauty even in the deep ugly, so I decide to look at her again and to listen to her without resisting any longer.

In my therapist's office, I explain about the Well-Woman. Ms. T is never surprised when a new character materializes for me. She seems to completely understand the world that I live in in my head and the characters who dwell there with me, and she does not attempt to reframe my experience into any other light than the one I present.

"She's arisen from the abyss," I say. "She seems unstoppable. Maybe I could have stopped her if we hadn't bought the house or if I hadn't quit my job or if I hadn't walked on the beach with Adam."

"No," she replies. "You could not have stopped her. It's her time. She's been emerging for years."

"Has she?"

"Yes." Ms. T's voice is calm. She is not frightened by what frightens me. "As I have told you, I've seen her before."

"She may destroy me," I lament.

"Yes. She very probably will destroy parts of you. But you'll live again."

I remain dubious, but nod amiably. I will depend upon the faith of others for now.

Back at the house, I stay away from the yard and the well for a few days. I begin to recall, however, a previous time, when I was very young, that the Well-Woman had access to both dry land and the deep waters. The traces in my memory are scant, but I can recount times at the trailer house of creating pretend dinners out of mud, swinging with imaginary friends and playing doctor with a little neighborhood pal, my senses fully intact and engaged. Those were the times about which my grandparents tell the stories of my curiosity. "She wasn't afraid of anything. She could spell M-I-S-S-I-S-S-I-P-P-I when she was two. She wanted to know about everything, always asking, 'What is it, Gampa?'" Those were times before anyone required me to be grown-up, before the parents realized their marriage would not last. It was before the house we lived in burned to the ground and before the stepfather came.

As each new event required me to protect myself from the grown-ups and their abuses, or as I realized how important it was to those around me that I be strong and "mature for my age," the Well-Woman descended into her retreat and rarely demanded attention until adolescence.

When I was in high-school and she had been long underwater, the Well-Woman beckoned me to the well many times. She came to me through my high school boyfriend, who was a soulish creature full of enjoyment of the senses without apology or regret. He was co-captain of the football team, a member of the theater troop, an avid reader, and a music lover. Many times, he tried to teach me to listen to the Well-Woman. Most potent are the memories of his attempts at interesting me in music. One late summer day we sat in his bedroom, surrounded by his hundreds of alphabetized record albums. He played one song after another for me of Genesis and Rush, pleading with me to feel the passion of the instruments, the voices, the words. But I could not hear. The messages from church, claiming that unsavory music could damage our chances at heaven, were already becoming imbedded.

And I could not handle his kisses. Too many forbidden things happened to my body and my heart when his breath came into contact with my own. Too many voices were bellowing at me from church and home: Don't touch. Don't smell. Don't look at this or that. Don't taste. Most of all, just don't make trouble.

I broke up with him at least four times before he entirely gave up on me. No laser show, no concert, no romantic walk under the stars or sweet, longing touch could break the lid on the well.

Even so, the Well-Woman was banging on the well-walls during these years, and I did sense her presence and hear the reverberating echoes of her pounding. In my creative writing classes or on stage in the theater, I took full breaths of pungent air. I was aware of a wildishness that could not be kept underground forever. My journals from this time period are filled with poetry and sad dirges. I carried a notebook with me everywhere so that I could write of images and feelings experienced in class, on the bus, at work, on the stage.

By this time, however, I had joined with a strict church that offered me a solid, clear set of guidelines for living, something greatly lacking in my family where I was already the cornerstone of stability for the other members.

Even my writing was discouraged in my religious community because grief and sorrow were considered ungodly and it was often my sadness of which I wrote. I soon learned to write only about joy and redemption. This gave my writing a false, unapproachable quality, and I eventually all but gave it up as an indulgence I could not afford without guilt.

Only in the theater could I be someone other than the dependable crutch people leaned on. There, both on stage and backstage, I could take on roles that were prohibited in other settings. On the stage, I was energized and stimulated. The tone of freedom that flooded that little theater left me feeling reproached by my conscience, but also unspeakably revived and restless, willing to risk and reveal more than the strictures of my religious and home life would allow.

Once, during a performance of a murder mystery, I rushed to the costume room for a change of clothing between scenes and found my old elementary school friend in there changing as well. He was half-undressed when I entered. I knew from the teachings I had been receiving at church that it would be "lascivious" (a word I'd heard for the first time the previous Sunday) to change in front of him, but there was no time for deliberation, so I shrugged at him and tore off my dress, hurrying into my next costume. This was one such moment, full of life to me—honesty and freedom from the religiously induced shyness, experienced in one fragment of an instant with no time for remorse. I rushed out and back onto the stage.

Now, Adam, I meet you in a costume room, of sorts. The disguises I was wearing a few months ago are removed. You are partly dressed. I am changing, but not hurriedly. We steal a few moments of honest touch before saying goodbye when I quit my job, but I ask you not to kiss me because I know that right now I don't have good defenses against either passion or guilt (I will rescind this request at some point, of course). In fact, I hold so still as you embrace me that I forget to breathe and nearly faint, something that has happened to me only twice before (once when

I had my wisdom teeth removed and once just after my first pelvic exam).

As I drive away from you, and over the next weeks, you and your touch are with me. My cravings are stronger, my fantasies more intrusive than ever in my life. Your face, which I could look at closely for only a short, joyful time, is before me at night and in the morning.

I realize I will be suspended in this miserable place of longing-but-not-having if I do not take steps to move forward. I know where to turn for guidance.

So, I go to the yard in my mind's eye, cross through the field and into the trees where the hidden well resides. I see her before I have fully approached. She remains in the position in which I left her, half in and half out of the water. It seems she will not ascend entirely without my consent or invitation. She is doing the oddest thing: fiber by fiber she is unraveling the crusted rope around the top of the rockery wall of the well. She shreds and yanks, sometimes with bloodied fingers, sometimes with her teeth. When I finally arrive to look her full in the face, I see that she is a mess of dried and sticky blood. She is determined to unravel that rope, to shred it into tiny, unrecognizable pieces, or she will die trying. But when she spots me, she stops her work. Her fierce gaze softens, and she offers me her hand. I take it and gently lift her from the well. She is at once totally weightless and solid through and through.

It is frightening to face oneself in this way. At close range, without the thick safety of my protective varnish, the laws of the church and the ways in which I have internalized them, I am unsure how to think of the Well-Woman. She is entirely undomesticated. Being shackled to the bottom of the reservoir has given her a great earthiness. She is moist and dirty. When she is entirely out of the well, I have my first opportunity to look full at her body. Strangely, her skin is not shriveled and shrunken as I would expect of one so long submerged. Instead, she is firm, shapely, and rounded. I want to touch her and see if she is as smooth as she appears, but I hardly feel I know her well enough for this indulgence. There are, to be sure, cuts and bruises on her thighs and forearms where her body has brushed up against the stones of the well wall. And her ankles are rubbed raw from the chafing of the shackles. Still, if it were not for the wan color of her skin, her figure would be pleasing to look at. As it stands, I am fascinated and cannot take my eyes away.

She takes my hand, and we walk in the direction of the house, her leading me. I would prefer to spend the day together outside in this yard, but she is insistent we go inside. All the while, as we walk, she moves her red lips, but no sound comes forth. At the threshold to the back of the house, she pauses, places her dirty, bloody hand on my face, looks into my eyes (I notice her eyes are brilliant blue with a glint of green around the edges) as if to pass some psychic message between us, and then moves through the door. I follow, dazed.

I find that I begin to hear her thoughts. Her lips still move, but no audible sound is being made. Some sort of thought transmission is taking place. *Surely this is not your home,* she says.

"Yes, this is where I live," I reply.

Through the kitchen and into the living room she wanders, taking in every picture, knickknack, and piece of furniture. She runs her had along my navy-blue sofa. *These are not your things.*

"They are," I protest.

She goes to the window and looks out at the hedge, the grass, the looming trees. *Where is the city?* she asks me.

"We live in the country," I say.

She turns to look at me in disbelief. *We live in the country? Impossible. You wanted to live in the center of the city when you were younger. I remember.* She looks hard at me, discerning something. Can she read my thoughts, too? Of course she can, I know at once. She knows them better than I. *Let me see the place where you write.*

We amble up the stairs to the tiny room I have fashioned as a writing room. My laptop sits open, the photos of Europe I took hang on the wall. She glances around at the furniture, the books, the print of *Her Cat* by Stephen Scott Young on the left wall. She nods. *This is better, but not complete. Why do you keep it so clean? Where are the scraps of paper with hand-copied quotes? Where are your messes? You love your messes.*

I feel bereft, criticized. I want to cry after hearing her complaints. Of course, she is right. I have cleaned up what would once have been scattered with incomplete ideas and half-finished projects. I believed everyone who told me to leave off starting something new until the old was finished and lost many new things along the way. The ideas for stories and memoirs are tucked neatly into file cabinets where they do not haunt and stalk me. I have moved in the ways I was supposed to move and have sacrificed, willingly but unthinkingly, the natural cycles and ways my soul is drawn to.

You call me. I have been waiting to hear from you, needing to hear your voice. You read me the poetry you have written, reflecting on our last experience together. It cuts through me. You write about our parting embrace. The "warmth above your knee" you speak of is the part of me that leads my journey, the place that has neither received nor given life until recently. How is it that you know these things? I tell you that no one has noticed this part of me before. You insist I should accept nothing less than to be noticed. And you remind me that you believe in me.

You have become a good liar, she says, gently. We still stand in my writing room. *You want truth, now, but it may cost you more than you are willing to pay.*

I nod. "I know. I don't know how to stop lying about who I am and what I want and what I feel."

You'll come with me to the well.

"To the well? I've just rescued you from the well. I don't want to get stuck down there." I am frightened and confused. The water in the well is rancid. I saw unidentifiable debris floating on the surface and even fancied I saw something swimming down there when I first gazed inside.

The well is not a place from which one needs rescuing, she says. *The shackles that held me at the bottom prevented me from coming to the surface to rescue you.* So, as usual, I am mistaken about who is the heroine and who is the damsel in distress. Always supposing myself the rescuer, I eventually find my own pain and need screaming out for attention. The Well-Woman recognizes this.

What she does next startles me. Her lips stop moving and she stares hard at my eyes, moving close to my face with her dirt-smudged, mud-infested head. It is not long before I see she means to kiss me. I draw away. "Oh my God, no," I say, disgusted.

She remains calm, unalarmed by my reaction. *If you are not stimulated by my sensuality, if you do not breathe my breath, you cannot live under the water or examine its contents. You have to taste the dirt that repels you in order to be prepared to dive into the truth-water.*

"I need time to think," I say.

The time for thinking is over. You've been thinking your whole life. It's the time to feel and to know.

I step away from her to look out the window. As I write each day, I look at the gardens the husband keeps. They are beautiful with nasturtium and clematis, rhododendrons, and bleeding hearts. But they are not my gardens. Then I close my eyes and see the well in the distance of my own inner yard. It is the only thing besides this room that is my own discovery since coming to this house, and I realize that while there may be dross in its waters, there may also be vital refreshment if I can go deep beyond the muck floating on the surface. So, I open my eyes and prepare to kiss the ugliness that has been offered to me.

When I turn from my reverie, the Well-Woman is no longer in the room with me. Frantic that I have missed my opportunity, I go searching for her. She is not downstairs in the white, lifeless kitchen, nor can I find her in the living room with the numb dé-cor. A peek into each bathroom and bedroom does not reveal her whereabouts. As I become desperate, fearing she has snuck away and that I will never know her breath, her sensuality, her truth, I hear an odd chawing noise coming from up the stairs. I follow this sound, listening carefully, trying to discern what could be causing it, and find her crouched down in my large, walk-in closet. This sound she is making is like an open-mouthed chewing—*chomp, swish, chomp.* It amazes me, as I peer closely, to see that she is indeed doing what I, at first glance, had perceived. She is eating my clothes.

"Please," I say, "stop." She has my red skirt in her hand and has already bitten into it, tearing a long piece off around the hem-line. She swallows.

You won't need these. Besides, they are not yours. They belong to all of the people around you—all but these. She points to indicate some selected pieces, which she has salvaged and arranged into a small pile on the floor. I go to them and rummage through, interested in what she has chosen to call my own. There are my blue jeans, of course, and the odd sweater or shirt, a few outfits purchased on a whim, a pair of black shoes, and then, a strange item I did not even recall having in my closet. There, amongst the cotton, lies my black prom dress.

I lift it from the floor. "My God. I haven't seen this in years." I hold it up to me. It is several sizes too large. I had been almost fifty pounds heavier when I wore it. "Why did you save this?" I ask her.

Remember when you wore it? Remember whom you chose as a date? I was so proud the day you asked Jay to take you to the prom. You did not wait to be asked. You did not consider that he was the boyfriend of a friend and the friend of your boyfriend. You had only two goals for that night: to be yourself and to enjoy yourself. Prom night was one of your most authentic experiences. That same night, I danced under the water until I was exhausted. When you finally arrived home at two o'clock in the morning I slept and dreamt of the future. You will wear this today. Put it on.

Curious about how I might look in the old thing now, I strip out of the clothes I am wearing and slip the prom dress over my head. My image in the full-length mirror on the back of the closet door is ridiculous.

I call to mind the details of making the dress. The mother and I had searched for and located a pattern and the yardage needed to make a dress I could dance in. I had not wanted a binding, overly long, pink gown like the other young women were wearing. She sewed that dress right up until Jay picked me up in his Dodge

Dart. As I departed the house and walked down the driveway, she was still basting in the last shoulder pad (which fell out later in the evening, at which point I simply removed the other one, as well).

The Well-Woman rises from her perch and walks a circle around me. *You are beautiful,* she says. And then she catches me in her embrace and kisses me, hard and full. I cannot breathe, at first. The taste of dirt and filth are gritty against my teeth, and I want her to release me, so I push at her, but she clutches me all the more tightly. Blood is rushing away from my head. I am suffocating. The taste of bile rises into my throat, and I know I will collapse if she does not let me go. Then suddenly, without warning . . . a breath. Deep and full, I breathe in through my mouth, her lips still pressed hard against mine. It is her breath I take in.

The time seems endless. Her kiss has some quality of the Everlasting in it. After I feel the deep breathing become regular and easy, I am surprised by the scant hint of sweetness in the taste of her mouth. The sensation increases in intensity the longer we are locked together. Before long, I crave the earthy taste of her and I will not let go of her body. I grasp her more tightly. My limbs begin to shake. Every place where I have skin tingles, longs for, is ravenous after her. The smell of mud in her hair entices me to touch it. I reach for her head and feel the twigs, the matting, the soggy mush and I cannot touch it enough, cannot emancipate her from my clutch. Just when I think my body can handle no more of my desire, she pulls away from me, but unlike the bitterness that comes of freeing oneself from a sexy embrace, I am relieved, the vehemence of our kiss having so penetrated my senses.

The Well-Woman lifts her arm from my hip and touches both my eyes at once with her hand. I close them.

We descend the stairs, exit the house, and make our way to the well, her leading me, as before. When we arrive, she insists we circle the well and observe the symbols on the outside of the wall. I ask her about the strangely familiar initials: I.F.T., C.M.M., and K.R.F.

These are the initials of your grandmothers and of your mother. They have scratched at the well trying to get in and have left their marks. Their well-women live in these waters with me. Ah, yes. Now I recognized the letters. It was the final initial in each set, the presence of the maiden name, that had thrown me off when I had first seen them.

"Did they get in? Did they swim in the water?"

I cannot tell you their stories. They do not belong to me. I can tell you that if you, yourself, swim in the waters you will find the courage to ask them each the questions that plague you. If they have swum here, they will answer you honestly. Then you will know.

"Should we go in now?" I inquire. I am anxious to do the thing I have been dreading.

Not yet. First we will remove the remaining rope along the edge of the well wall. It must be unraveled completely and discarded in shreds before we can enter.

"But won't we cut ourselves on the rocks if the rope is removed?" I ask. I am the one everyone knows who has never had stitches or a bloody nose or a broken bone. I dislike risking injury and do not relish the idea that I will most certainly be cut if I climb over the unprotected wall into the truth-water.

Yes, she answers. *You will be cut, many times. The way to truthfulness is not clean and tidy like your writing room. It is bloody and painful. Remember Christ? Freedom requires injury. We will begin unraveling where I left off, here.* She indicates the spot on the rope where she had been picking when I came to her and offered her my hand.

We spend the better part of the day unraveling the rope and ripping it away from the top of the wall. The work goes faster with the two of us working together than it did when she worked alone, but it is, nevertheless, a painstaking process. She insists that I give a title to each shard that is freed from the whole. She depends on me to find the names.

"I call this piece of the protective rope 'Silently Doing What is Asked,' and this piece will be 'Keeping Small Talk Going for Hours.'"

Yes. Good. And what of this long, thick piece I have just torn away? she asks.

"I need to think awhile on that one," I reply. It is a long stretch of rope, the length of my arm, and thick. It must have a significant name. All at once, I know. "It must be 'Secretly Crying Myself to Sleep.'" I have always kept my tears a secret, knowing the mother, the brothers, the husband could not handle my weeping.

Ah, yes. This has kept you out of the well, she reasons. You have cried secretly your whole life, until lately. Only recently have you let others see your deep, deep grief. And some have been still and let you cry, but others have walked away or tried to stop the flow.

We work on and on, naming the pieces and discarding them, until there is only one stubborn portion remaining. Together we rip at it, attempting to tear it into small strips, but it will not come apart. We decide to try to pry it loose intact, but it is firmly attached to the wall, and we get the fibers under our fingernails. I cut my forearm on one of the exposed stones no longer protected by braiding. It is a fairly deep cut, approximately two inches long, but it has not hit any veins or arteries, so it bleeds slowly and consistently. It may need stitches, yet I am unwilling to break up my quest by getting medical attention.

The Well-Woman sees my blood and gets an idea. *Bleed on the rope, she commands. Let's soften it with your blood.*

Willing to try anything at this point, I position my arm above the rope and squeeze the blood over its crusted threads. Upon contact with the red liquid, the rope thickens and softens, like a dried sponge soaking in water. We are easily able to lift it from the wall in one piece after this, without further injury.

What is its name? the Well-Woman asks me.

There is such an odd sensation in my stomach as she asks me this. I know its name, but I am not at all certain if I can say it aloud. This last strand has been crusted to the wall for decades and may have kept both the matriarchs of my family and myself from either getting wounded at the well or from entering it. It has fallen upon me to tear it away and to name it.

Speak it, she admonishes. *It has to be said.*

So, I open my mouth to name the rope. My lips move without sound like those menstrual-red lips of the Well-Woman. Over and over again, I mouth the words of the name of the largest piece of rope, but still no voice issues forth. The nausea increases. My tongue feels large and useless.

But then I hear a noise. It is raspy and crackling, like the sound of someone speaking in the morning for the first time. It is the voice of the Well-Woman. She speaks in unison with the movement of my own lips. My thoughts and her speech are merging into one statement in this moment as they have done all along, but this time she is the audible one.

"Being unknown, being unseen. Being unknown, being unseen. Being unknown, being unseen." She speaks the words more loudly and smoothly with each repetition. *"Being unknown, being unseen . . ."*

The sensation in my stomach rises into my chest as she continues to repeat the phrases I mouth. It comes up into my throat. My lips continue to move; her voice continues to speak. *"Being unknown, being unseen. Being unknown . . ."* I cannot contain my insides any longer. In a repulsive combination of sobbing and retching, I vomit the contents of my stomach onto the cement floor that forms the base of the well. My cramping is laborious. The sensation of each heave starts in my womb and moves upwards in increments through each section of my torso: stomach, chest, throat. Finally, the contents come through my mouth.

I weep, attempting to catch my breath between each new wave. When, finally, there is nothing more to be ejected from my body, I sit, leaning against the well where the mothers of my family have carved their initials, and I rest.

As I am about to plunge into the well, dear one, you go away for the weekend. I think of you kayaking in the wilderness with the people you love and trust, and I wonder if you are finding what you hoped you would discover out in the deep. Is there peace? Unity? Space to grieve? It seems a bizarre parallel that you trek through the water, powered by your own strength against the oars, just as I begin my journey inward, powered by nothing but need for truth and change. I regret that we don't travel together, but I think of the phrase "deep calling to deep," a Biblical quote meant (I have been taught) to represent the longing humans have to know God. I now consider the possibility that this idea describes nothing more than the mystical connections the universe sometimes provides between two minds. You and I do, indeed, travel together, only not in the conventional way just now.

I rise, lift my skirt, and throw my right leg over the edge of the well. My thigh receives a gash from a sharp stone in the wall. It stings like hell and makes me think better of raising my skirt before bringing my other leg along. The cumbersome material of the too-big prom dress may come in handy. I tuck the black folds under my left leg and swing it in line with the right. Without my expecting it, the Well-Woman gives me a shove from behind, and I fall awkwardly into the well. Then, with the graceful movement of someone who is completely prepared for her task, she dives in after me and pulls me fully under the water.

I gasp.

"Breathe easily," she says to me.

I try again and find that, yes, my lungs are malleable, willing to accept this kind of breathing. The water is cool and, although it is remarkably dark to my unadjusted eyes, and although there is debris and refuse floating beside us, it is also sweeter to the taste than I had imagined it would be and refreshing against my wounds.

"What do we do now that we're down here," I wonder.

"We have an important task. There are some items here you need to recover from the bottom and take back with you to the upper world. And we have housework to do. This well has not been cleaned for a very long time. We will do it together."

As my eyes adjust to the murkiness and darkness of being far below the reach of sunlight, I am struck by the depth and breadth of the well. I suppose I had imagined it would be as narrow as the upper chamber all the way to the bottom, but I find there is ample room for moving about once one is below the construct of the wall. It is much like an underground lake. In fact, I cannot see the boundaries of it from where I presently swim. Is it possible that this well is limitless, infinite? Or are there banks along some unseen edges that I may crash into, unsuspecting and unprepared?

The Well-Woman does not reveal to me the size of the reservoir. Now that we are in the truth-waters, she seems unlikely to answer any queries directly. Instead, when I communicate some wondering, some ponderance, she often catches my eye, briefly, and then indicates the surroundings with a nod from her head as if to say, *"Look around you. The answer is here."* This annoys me because I am unused to swimming in deep water without knowing where solid ground is. I prefer not to feel ambivalent or surprised. Unopened Christmas presents, unanswered questions, and deep waters without shores unnerve me. I am reminded of snorkeling in Hawaii and how, once, I swam further from the shore than I had meant to. The reef I had been exploring dropped away and the water, so blue and shiny up against the sand, became darkly ominous. I had panicked and turned back to the beach as quickly as possible, afraid, I suppose, of encountering monsters of some kind in the reef-less, bottomless ocean, all by myself. The Well-Woman appears to be at home in this and all kinds of ambiguity.

The odd thing about the water in the well is its variable consistency. This underground lake is seemingly divided into sections, like large rooms. One section I swim through contains the cleanest, most enriching cool water. I take in the rejuvenation by breathing in the water intentionally and completely. I feel washed, cleansed, renewed as I do so. This is the feeling I have sought many times in the church revival meetings I attended for years, this sense of "all-is-well." I think of the lyrics to a hymn sung every Sunday at the first little Baptist church I ever attended. It asserts, "When peace, like a river, attendeth my way, / When sorrow, like sea-billows roll, / Whatever my lot, thou hast taught me to say/ It is well. It is well with my soul." This is the sense I have in the pure water. It is well with my soul. After resurfacing from such water, I liken my experience to the symbol of baptism. Buried and dead to the old life, I am resurrected anew.

But as I swim on in the seemingly endless hidden lake, I come to waters of other textures and temperatures. It becomes most difficult for me to breathe in the places where murkiness and bog dominate the conditions. I have never been easy with muck. Once or twice, I feel distressed and begin to flail, choke in the mud, and search with my feet for something solid on which to stand. There is nothing concrete nearby to stabilize me, but the Well-Woman is never far away. She takes my arm and steadies me. In just one of these thick places, the thickest of this venture so far, she says, "*Here we will begin to sort through the debris. We'll throw some things out and take some things back to land with us.*" And our work begins.

The next morning, I receive a telephone call from the mother. She wants to talk of my stepfather's mental illness. I am the resident expert on relationships and mental health, naturally. The oldest child, the only daughter, the most well-put-together (they think), and the one with the most education, I am the perfect candidate to turn to for sympathy and support. All the members of my family have done it at one time or another. As for myself, I turn outside of the family for what I need. I think of you, Adam, looking into my eyes and seeing me. And I think of how you have allowed me to see you, too. These kinds of connections are becoming increasingly frequent in my life. There is a circle around me of individuals who listen until the ends of my sentences and ask me questions as if interested in what I have to say. I'm finding friends who give me access to their own dark domains without requiring me to fix or heal (and oddly enough healing occurs, sometimes). You are one such friend. Still, I cannot seem to establish new patterns with some people in my life. I turn to assume the usual position with the mother—arms open toward her, but heart closed off to myself. This time, however, my stance is tentative; there is another pose taking shape as she begins to speak.

"He was so unaccountably upset because he had lost his shoes and couldn't find them before church. He wasn't throwing a temper tantrum, but he was just so frustrated that he picked up the fan—you know that big fan we have in our bedroom—and threw it against the wall. It definitely was not a temper tantrum, but he was so thoroughly embarrassed after he had done it, chagrined really. I told him, 'It's okay. Don't worry. It's not a big deal.'"

On she drones, repeating several times that "it was not a temper tantrum" until I feel the blood rushing through my heart more rapidly each time the phrase is uttered. The silence of years and years of listening to her marital problems or her sicknesses or his sicknesses, without regard to my own grief-filled memories of childhood or my own sensitivities, suddenly unstops and I interrupt her, something I was taught not to do and have rarely done to anyone.

"It was a temper tantrum," I say. My heart is quieted. I am momentarily calm, like those stand-still moments before the torrential rains begin.

"No. It was just an anxiety attack," she says.

"No. It was violence," I say. "It was violence just like when I was a child."

"No. You misunderstand my story. It wasn't like that." She chuckles. Her affect, that of a mother telling the cute tale of her toddler's misbehaviors, infuriates me.

"No. It was violence. Like the times he hit me for not moving fast enough on my chores. Like the time he knocked you to the ground with the back of his forearm. Like the time he used to pin brother to the wall with his pointy finger pounding into brother's tiny chest. It's violence like that." And then suddenly I cannot stop myself. I go on and on about my grievances against her and her sick relationship and their illnesses and mental health problems, for which they do not seek any help beyond medication. "And another thing . . . and another thing . . . and another thing . . ." Until my head begins to ache with the relief of it all.

Finally, I say the one thing which I have held most tightly for fifteen years. I speak of the secret pain, the worst betrayal she and the stepfather ever transgressed against me. I pour it out like curdled milk, holding back none of my thoughts, regurgitating every detail with the potency of my truth. When I am finished, I wait for her response. The waiting goes on for a metaphorical lifetime, for about thirty-four years.

Finally, she speaks. "You still think that really happened?" she asks.

I pause, dumbfounded by her reply.

I cannot help myself. I begin to laugh at her question. I had assumed that she, like me, was pretending the terrible event had not happened as a way of keeping the tentative peace between us. Now I find she has been settled into authentic denial for many years. "Yes," I say and breathe.

"No," she says.

"Yes. Yes," I say.

Although I am shocked by her disaffirmation of reality, I am equally dismayed at my own failure to recognize and acknowledge the mother's true state. For years upon end, I have maintained a dishonest relationship with her, saying to myself, "It's not so bad.

She has a lot on the ball. She's quirky, to be sure, but she is basically pretty aware of what has happened to me, to the brothers." Like standing under a flock of birds and not expecting to get shit on, I have continued a perfunctory relationship with the mother never anticipating that her lack of enlightenment would run up hard against my growing awareness. Bam!

And still, the Well-Woman treads water, comfortable with the mess, sorting through the dregs, throwing this out, keeping that for later.

The ability to speak, as in my conversation with the mother, is one of the skills she insists I take with me when I surface. In some of the murkiest water, I find where this ability, once known to me, instinctually, in those early encounters with the well in Brier-Rose, had gone to. The Well-Woman takes me through an underground tunnel of memories, the walls of which are lined with books, tattered, well-handled volumes without titles on their spines.

"What are these?" I ask.

"Choose a volume from the wall and find out," she replies.

I choose one near the tunnel entrance. It is a journal—the one I kept in junior high, when I first began both my commitment to my art and my sexual development. I open it and read and am surprised to find pages written as an ode to young lust and desire for enduring connections with other young people.

I read aloud for the Well-Woman to hear, "In my dream I feel no guilt. In my open hideaway, I express my yearning without words." I wonder what I knew of "yearning" then that I have now forgotten.

"You were only thirteen years-old when you wrote that," she says pensively. *"Sad that the longings of which you wrote became subverted. But I am here now, at last."*

Yes. I'm sad that my development in this regard was arrested for two decades, but I am also excited that this part of me is not dead.

I read through this early volume languidly before I finally replace it and choose another, more recent one. This next book is the one I kept the year I met and married the husband. I page through, turning slowly over the implications of what I am reading. The contrast with the earlier journal is so startling. Here I am struck and appalled by the lies it contains. I wrote of love and joy and godliness when I clearly remember experiencing guilt and doubt and lust. I was writing what I believed I was required to feel. The pretending had infiltrated even my own thoughts by this time, and I had become almost entirely incapable of being honest with myself.

So it is the knowledge that I have been unendingly accommodating religious and familial expectations that I must take with me onto dry land. I swallow as much of the truth-water as I can contain, both the fresh and the muddy and then I surface.

Above ground, a few weeks after the Well-Woman's reemergence, an outing with "friends" is planned. I am to go to dinner at a noisy restaurant where the food is copious, if not particularly interesting or refined. The friends in question are not my people, they belong to the husband.

I know before going that I will be required to make small talk and to add interesting tidbits to a conversation I will care nothing. Still, I am truly taken aback when I find myself unable to perform my tasks with the usual ease and willingness I typically exhibit. It seems the Well-Woman has little patience for boredom and social requirements. She asserts herself into the conversation at unexpected moments and I am unable to quiet her.

When we arrive, the restaurant is bustling. Diners are being seated, served, and ushered out the door in a twirling, stormy rush of human activity that disturbs me. The couple we are meeting is sitting in a booth, snuggled together like children sharing a secret. *"Too close,"* the Well-Woman says. *"They look like one person with two heads."* She has become petulant with extended exposure to air.

Shut up, I think. *Don't criticize.*

We slide in across from them and greet them each by name and ask the usual questions about traffic and trouble finding the restaurant. Then there is a long, uncomfortable silence. Silences distress me. *"Well, don't expect me to carry the conversation",* the Well-Woman says to me. *"If you people don't have anything to say to one another, too bad. Sit here in silence all night, you inarticulate fools. I don't give a damn."* Meanwhile, I search my mind for something to say and study the menu with a perfectly pathological intensity. I used to be excellent at this kind of thing. I could keep a nonsensical conversation going when everyone else in the circle was at a loss for finding a mutually interesting topic. I know what these people are interested in: baseball, computers, workplace politics. *"Don't say a word",* the Well-Woman warns me. *"If we talk about baseball or computers, I'm taking us out of here."* I know I would be embarrassed if the Well-Woman marched me out of the restaurant because she was bored with the conversation, so I stay quiet. She neither wants me to take responsibility for getting a topic going, nor does she want me to take part in talking about anything that does not interest her. My own discomfort rises. What if no one else takes the lead? What if we sit here staring at one another for two hours? God, where is our waiter?

I excuse myself to go to the restroom. In the stall, I go to the well and look down inside. "Hey," I beckon. "What do you want me to do? I've got to talk about something. I'm expected to participate, you know."

"I don't care. I don't like these people. They bore me. They've always bored me."

"But I have responsibilities here. You can't boycott people because they bore you."

"I can. Too bad for you if you can't," she retorts.

"So I should just sit in the booth and stare at my food?"

"Do what you want." She gives me a significant stare.

Do what I want? What do I want? My God, I think, I could do what I want? I lean against the side of the stall trying to determine what it is I might want. It comes to me. I want to be out for a glass of wine with a friend. I want to be talking about the book I am reading and my ideas for starting a business. And then I want to rent a video of a foreign film I recently heard about and for my friend and me to go back to her place and watch it together. I don't want to be here with these people at all. But I do not think I have the courage to do something about it. It would be so utterly inappropriate to say I needed to leave.

"I can't," I say.

"Perhaps tonight you can't, but someday soon you will."

"I have to get back." I open the stall and see a line of women waiting against the wall for an available toilet. I fancy they are giving me inquiring stares and wonder if they have overheard my conversation or if they are merely desperate to get into the stalls in order to have similar discussions with their own well-women.

Back at the booth, they are talking about baseball. The Well-Woman grips me by the leg and tries to pull me around, toward the restaurant door. *"I'm going now!"* she shouts.

But I stand firm. "No," I say.

"What?" The husband asks. "'No' what?"

I hadn't realized I had spoken aloud.

"No reason to get up. I'll sit on the outside of the booth," I say. It seems like a good recovery to me, but I can feel the flush in my face. My body is absolutely in a battle, like Jacob's struggle with the angel, and I am exhausted. I expect I will receive a wound to my hip before the night is over.

The next day I burn your poetry as you requested, Adam, down by the well. I kiss each gift one by one and then light it afire in the flame of the candle I have burning beside me. I place the ashes in a porcelain flowerpot. When all are burned beyond recognition, I scoop water from the well with my hand, cutting my forearm, slightly, on the jagged rocks around the top of the wall. I mingle the ashes, water, and blood together in the pot, swishing them around until I cannot tell one from the other—it's just a gray mixture.

I do this out of loyalty to you. You are aware, I am sure, that many important things in my life have burned to cinders—literally and otherwise. In fact, much more than poetry is burning in my life at this time. It seems there is a cremation of my very self occurring.

The will to please others burns.

The desire to follow long-trodden moral pathways burns.

Devotion to vows made in my youth burns.

Even five percent of my body weight burns away.

All these ashes make the well-water rich.

I look into the grayness of the burnt-up poetry and see in it your vision of me—sexy, desired, uninhibited, intelligent, funny, and capable. My thirst to take these qualities into myself becomes unyielding and in a moment of delinquent judgment, I lift the flowerpot to my lips and drink several long gulps of the potion made out of your words.

Having broken the long silence within one of my most intense relationships, I find that the silence which peppers the flavor of my other connections is less viable, more fragile. I regularly hear the sounds of splashing and laughter coming from the center of my body. It does not take me long to realize that speaking my truth once will not be enough to satisfy this strange friend I have made. In fact, not a fortnight goes by before she is asking for yet more truth.

I am at the baseball park watching grown men get paid millions of dollars for playing a game they love to play. Inside of me, I can hear her pounding on the cavity of my chest. I am not entirely uncertain what she may want. She is insistent and violent, really. I want to silence her, shut her up, re-shackle her to the bottom of the well, but she remains incredibly tenacious and will not be enslaved, no matter how I coerce her. *Can you not silence yourself for a few weeks until the summer is over, or until after Christmas?* I plead with her, silently. No one seems aware of this argument going on inside of me. Only I experience it as clamorous and unceasing.

While the husband is in the restroom and forty-five thousand other fans engage in the game as it unfolds on the field, I close my eyes and go into the well. I stand on the edge and dive in without hesitation, for I am experienced at breathing in the water by now.

I find her and take hold of her hand. It takes a moment in the water before we can get turned round to face one another. "What is it? What should I do? What would you have me do? I want to be full of you, but I'm afraid."

She pulls me near and enfolds me in her moist, gritty embrace and speaks into my ear, gently. *"You must speak the truth. You must take the truth-water out of the well onto dry land."*

I begin to cry. How many years have I called off what wanted to come out of my mouth? How many times have I contained the truth-water, plugged up the holes through which it might leak and silenced my most important words? I begin to reflect on these times and bitter water deluges my thoughts.

There was the time I was put on restriction for twelve weeks for trying to talk to the stepfather about my broken stereo. There was the time I ran away, down the street, and came home an hour later to speak with the mother about what was bothering me. She told me to stop being foolish and to go to bed. There were the numerous times the stepfather stood beside me in the kitchen, badgering me as I washed each dish, returning one after another to the dishwater, having declared the cleaning "not good enough." There was the first time (and the second and the third) I put off vacation for a soft-ball tournament, and the moment I finally gave up the idea of being a missionary because the husband did not want to go with me. There have been the thousand times someone has called me "good," and I have been unable to slough off the burden of being the perfect one. There have been the million times I have wanted to say, "No," and have said, "Yes, thank you," instead. There has been the moment by moment small talk made in my marriage when I could talk of "this and that" no longer, but have kept going and going, unable to say, "If you can't talk to me of poetry or philosophy or religion or feelings or yourself or myself, then leave me alone." There were the childhood conversations in which the mother cried and asked me to support her intentions of bringing the stepfather back into my house after he had abused and cheated on her. There were my wedding vows in which I promised to give up my name for the husband's name, even though I did not want to lose my identity or my name into his. There have been the friendships with needy individuals which have sucked my soul away from me and left me as parched as sub-Saharan Africa. There were the tithes given unquestioningly and the sermons integrated into my personal theology without doubt or argument. There have been the rules restricting my intake of music, movies, alcohol, and sex, restricting my participation in particular literature, educational experiences, spiritual exercises, types of jokes, friends who embrace different belief systems, fantasies, and dreams that push "acceptable" limits.

These examples and others move through my mind rapidly. The silence has been rampant, fanning out into all of my most significant relationships. I never objected to the injustices against me, or, if I did, these objections were not given credence. And now this silence is squeezing so tightly it threatens to cut off my circulation.

"Yes. You must speak."

There are many individuals in my life who will not believe that my voice has been silenced. I write and I speak proficiently. I am articulate, even talkative. But I have not spoken, not really.

"Yes. You must speak," she says to me. "You must risk the consequences. You will open your mouth, and as you speak the hard truths of your well, you will learn what they are."

I open my eyes and the baseball game continues. No one seems to notice that the Well-Woman is present. The husband returns with his beer and French fries. He sees nothing different as he looks at me.

Suddenly, I can stay no longer. "Can we talk for a while when we get home?" I ask.

"We can," he tells me.

On the way home you call me. The husband and I have driven to the ball field separately, so I am alone in the car when my cell phone rings. Our voices meet. I want very much to be medicated by your conversation, by you, my dear. I had known you would call, as I have known many times before. I want to tell you a time and a place to meet, so you can take me away from everything, but I feel that I have an important task ahead of me and must not be distracted just now. I hear the Well-Woman saying, as she has said before, "Do what you want." You've been with me at the edge of this well all along, and I would like you to come in deeper, but you have your own reasons for being reluctant to do so. When you are in my thoughts, she gains strength. I'm glad you called.

Inside, we sit. I begin to speak. "I don't want to be married anymore. I've felt this way for a long time but have never told you. I didn't want to hurt you, and I don't want to hurt you now, but there is a pounding in my chest, a shaking inside of me for the truth to be told." I tell the husband that I have been holding onto a thinly constructed thread of attachment, which has kept me in place for these eleven years but will hold me no longer. I tell him that if I had not been able to distract myself from my disengagement by going to on my mission trip to Africa, I would have left him seven years ago. If I had not gone to graduate school, I would have left him three years ago. These things kept me from inquiring about my loneliness. Buying this house and quitting my job have taken from me what sustains me, and the marriage is not enough. I tell him that I cannot take care of his feelings anymore. I explain that I have stayed because I was afraid God would send me to hell if I left and because I did not want him to suffer and because my family would be so very disappointed in me if I was unable to make this marriage work. I note that these are not good reasons for me to stay anymore.

I have said it. All of it. I wait. There is silence.

He is perfectly still for a great length of time. Still, I wait. I have softened nothing, as I normally would. I have not told partial lies to make him feel better.

Suddenly, he gets up and goes away. I hear him cry.

My God, the weight of that cry is like the weight of a powerful wind. It nearly takes me off my feet, but it does not knock me over. I have cried for several years and carried the monstrous burden of being the only one on the planet to know my truth. And then I began to tell of my burden to a few of the most trusted people in my life and the burden was identified and cared for, a little, but still, I carried it.

Now I have spoken of this burden to one of the people who has most colluded with me in creating it, just as I spoke with the mother about my other great silence.

The allayment of some unnamed-but-ever-present tension is almost tangible. I am released further from Façade and Pretense, just as the Well-Woman was released from her fetters only a few weeks ago.

While the Well-Woman gains a clearer voice, and as I struggle to breathe in the mud, you and I begin to sort out the truths between us, as well. Sometimes you are afraid of me, of my feelings, you say. Sometimes we say goodbye, meaning to part permanently, yet we share not only mutual relationships, but also, it seems, some kind of mystical connection that calls us back. We each make our attempts at being sensible, reasonable, logical. We know things on more than one level and want to make space for all that exists in our individual lives and in the life we share, somewhat secretly. I am unpredictable—no longer restrained. The dream-cat has escaped from the house and is slowly making her way across the freeway. I am not benign anymore—not safe, Adam. Remember this. Once you were afraid of being unsafe for me and now I am the wildcard.

Sometimes you run away, wisely.

We keep to ourselves, not telling others of our private affinity.

The Well-Woman remains peaceful, reminding me that her existence is not dependent on you. She has been nourished and catalyzed by your presence but is entirely independent. She reminds me of a portion of another T.S. Elliot poem: "I said to my soul, be still, and wait without hope/ for hope would be hope for the wrong thing; wait without love/ for love would be love of the wrong thing; there is yet faith/ But the faith and the love and hope are all in the waiting." She remains in the tension between loving and not loving, hoping and not hoping. I learn from her. I breathe in the mud, sputtering and choking, knowing that no one in my life will fit nicely into my former categories. You and I, and the husband and the mother and all the others who are touched (directly and peripherally) by her truth and her patient faith begin to defy the neat boxes I have kept for the people in my life.

I continue to speak my truths to others, little by little. As I have lost my capacity for mind-reading, I fail to alter my delivery based on how each person may respond as I explain that I will be leaving my marriage. Some people ask how I am doing, others grill me with questions, but with each new telling, the Well-Woman gains more control over my responses. I find phrases like "I'm not going to talk about that right now" siphoning through my lips.

One friend tells me how angry she was when she learned of my decision to move out of the new house. "You're God's witness to unsaved family and friends. What're you doing?" she asks.

I sit, silent for a long moment. But this is not the silence of former times. This is the silence of choice. How shall I choose to respond? I consult the Well-Woman (quickly now—no need to find a restroom anymore). She advises a calm reply.

"I don't think I will try to explain it to you," I begin. "I'll call you if I want to talk to you about it."

With each interaction I feel less like justifying myself and more like I have the right to make my life what I want it to be.

Years ago, when I was part of a very rigid religious community, we practiced something we called "living by faith." The premise of this practice was that one was to seek God for a direction in one's life and then, to follow it, regardless of available resources or practical considerations. I, myself, flew to France and stayed for four months without any money whatsoever. If one had enough faith in God and the path he had revealed, all that was needed would be supplied, miraculously.

I have long since dismissed this way of living as irresponsible, not to mention magical. But now I find myself needing a faith that looks much the same as that magical way of a previous time. I have nothing but my car and a few bags of necessities. I have no job, no family member who knows of the emergence of the Well-Woman, and no clear sense of direction or purpose.

On the day I choose to leave, I drive away from the house, stunned by the absolute disregard I am exhibiting for everything

I have stood for. Where will I go? I pull over to the side of the road and go into the well.

The well water is very dark today. It reeks of dead things, and, in fact, I see the carcasses of familiar companions float past me as I search for the Well-Woman. I see the Fat Man who has often sat or jumped on my chest when I have considered breaking a rule. He is still living, but I can see he is gasping; the well-water is too rich for him. I see the frightened child who has waved her sword and shouted warnings at me when I have thought of exploring my sexuality in some new way. She is still too frail for the waters. I give her a push up to the surface so she can wait for me on dry land.

I swim past these and other apparitions, calling to the Well-Woman. I am in dismay, unable to understand why she would not be readily available for me, though by now I know that she is not motherly and does not coddle or comfort. Still, she is usually at hand to give an opinion or to make a demand on her own behalf. Deeper and deeper I swim. The darkness increases.

Finally, I see a shadow. Or rather, I see two shadows. They seem to be dancing, if that is possible in the water. There is a swaying and undulating movement. One spins the other confidently, as if this dance has been rehearsed. I float closer, curiosity gaining strength. Who is in the well with the Well-Woman? Who is taking her attention so fully away from what is happening above ground, especially during such a momentous day as this has been for me?

Slowly, as I am near enough, the Well-Woman comes into focus, but the other figure remains shadowy and elusive. She is naked, as always. Her white body arches and dips and swishes while the Other Shadow, who I spontaneously understand to be Divinity making a visitation, leads her this way and that. I am drawn to their movements, but embarrassed that I am observing an intimacy into which I have not been invited.

So, I tread water some respectable distance away, gawking and breathing in the stench. How can they dance with such putridity so nearby? They seem not to notice. The longer I remain still, observing, the quieter my thoughts become. I can hear the sound of some whispered conversation between the swirling figures. I strain to listen, swimming only slightly closer, still fearing I will be discovered.

"She is frightened of you," I hear the Well-Woman saying.

"Yes," the Shadow replies. Nothing more.

"Shall we invite her into the dance?" she asks.

"Yes."

"Do you think she will come?"

"Not yet. Sometime soon," the Shadow says.

I want very much to join the dance, but I fear being scoffed at for not understanding the rhythm. I don't know the Shadow's disposition toward me yet, and I cannot risk being rejected. I ought to know by now that the Well-Woman would never consort with a character who would treat me with the kind of disdain I expect from Divinity, but there is only a little real faith in me just now. So I turn and swim away, vowing to come often and watch the dance from a distance. I'll memorize the movements before I risk soliciting an invitation to join them.

I do begin to dance, eventually. When this happens, I realize that the Well-Woman has begun to infuse me. She has slit an opening in my back and climbed inside of me, filling my arms and legs and belly with her gritty energy. When I swim in the well-water nowadays, I no longer see her face to face as I did in the beginning. I see her, instead, reflected back to me in the eyes of the Shadow figure as we do our swim-dance. Yes, I dance naked with the Shadow now. We swirl and convulse. Someone watching might well wonder if we are wrestling—and it is the dance of adversaries that we do, but of adversaries who know each other intimately.

On one particular day, our swirling movement stays with me long after my morning meditation. I go to a job interview in the morning at the home of a man who runs his business out of his condominium. I have verified with mutual acquaintances that this man and his situation are safe, but once I arrive at the door I am further reassured, intuitively, that I am in no danger.

For one hour, D interviews me and tells me about his agency. He is looking for someone to take on a few hours of work each week. I sit without anxiety throughout the entire conversation. In fact, although D would have no way of knowing it, I am letting the Well-Woman participate in this conversation while I merely lean into his leather chair and watch her proceed.

She is smooth and confident. "Yes. That sounds interesting. I can do that. I can start as soon as possible," she says. She goes on to enumerate my strengths and to tell D that he would be sorry to miss an opportunity to work with me.

I wonder if she might be going a little overboard and am afraid she may lose me the job, but I have had such little success finding employment for myself that I do not interfere.

D seems enchanted with her. He smiles that amused and cu-rious smile men make when they are not sure who is in charge of an interaction they expected to control.

"Do you make a good living at this?" I hear her ask. I wince. As in many other situations, I would like to silence her; she can be so terribly forward at times, but I have learned that it is fruitless to take over when she has set her mind on some direction. Her long imprisonment has rendered her insensible to the numerous possible connotations of some of her behaviors. She does not know that direct questions are considered rude or intrusive.

I watch D's face for disapproval, but because of my weakened mind-reading abilities, I see nothing.

"It makes me enough money to do what I really love to do," he answers.

"What would that be?" she inquires.

"Tango dancing," he says.

The Well-Woman laughs uproariously. I have to admit I find the image of this little man doing the Tango rather unlikely, too, but it does not seem prudent to laugh at him just now.

"I've had a few tango lessons myself," she spouts. My God, she is inviting disaster. I can feel it.

"Have you?" he asks. "Let's see what you can do."

No, I say to her internally. *I am not dancing with this stranger in his living room to get a job.*

Do what you please. I'm going to have some fun so this will all be worth something even if you don't get the job, she says back to me, quietly. I hope he doesn't hear our conversation.

I doubt he does because the little man is already moving toward the living room and popping a CD into his sound system. I remain seated, struggling briefly before giving in. "What the hell," I say and rise to do the first Tango I have ever danced at a job interview.

I move into an apartment. It is too close to you, you say. I may disrupt your life in some way. You wonder if you can trust yourself (to love me less when I am this close? to stop yourself from being in my life?). The intensity of our connection threatens to split you in half between the reality of the life you live and the fantasy of experiencing life with the Well-Woman. But life with the Well-Woman cannot be kept secret, Adam. She does not like to be held underground, but instead demands to be acknowledged—free to come and go as she pleases.

I spend more time in the well each day. We continue to sort, and I continue to know and enjoy the companionship of the Well-Woman. It is good she is available to me day and night because I have a daunting process ahead of me. I must tell the important people in my life about my choice to leave my former life, and I must introduce them to the Well-Woman. Naturally, they will think I am crazy.

I reflect on the dream I had of my cat/snake attempting to cross the freeway. The symbol of the danger of getting to the other side of the highway becomes clear to me. I will face the most precarious task of my life: I will disappoint those I have sought to please. I will look at my failures and will say that I do not care what they want of me but that I intend on following my own will.

I get the job and buy a red car and a red sofa. I paint the walls of my apartment orange and begin to search for wall-hangings that will please the Well-Woman. It is good that I have provided a space for us where we can be comfortable because the sorting and categorizing we do becomes very intense, and I am glad we are alone together as we rifle through every element of my life. In fact, the joy I felt at one point in my new acquaintance with the Well-Woman is replaced by a thick, bluish grief.

Under the water, I catch memories floating past. I hold each in my hands with a measure of tenderness and regret, and I weep. For every failure of my own and for every rejection by someone in my life, I send a cry into the universe. I fill the waters with the truth of my sadness. Deeper and deeper I swim into the losses of a lifetime. I fear the well is bottomless, that there will be no end to my mourning.

This is where I am now—in my apartment with the loneliness I have kept at bay until now. It is a painful release to be feeling it. It runs like a hot wire through the middle of my body, sending jolts that threaten to burn me up. I have the understanding that I will be here in this place for a long time and will need to look to the Well-Woman for patience and for hope for the future.

You, Adam, are among the losses I grieve. Could you have had any idea how to heart I would take every word you speak . . . every touch? At first, by opening yourself so freely, you helped me give birth to the Well-Woman and later, when you pulled away from me, you pressed the button that released the dammed-up grief I was hiding from myself and the rest of the world. There is nothing left of my old pretending self left of me. I will not be able to play one part on the outside while living another reality down in the well.

We have said to each other that the Well-Woman would have found a way to emerge without you walking on the beach with me those months ago, and I believe this to be true. The storm of sadness that overtakes me these days would have come to pass without you, as well, but these things did not occur in your absence. You have watched it all from a safe distance.

The grief alternates between being overwhelming and manageable. During a reprieve from the grief that has lasted long enough for me to begin to hope I am through the worst of it, Adam tells me he will arrive in the evening and knock on my door, accompanied by a bottle of wine.

The Well-Woman and I have been discussing what to make of men, lately. On this subject we often go our separate ways for a while, not much agreeing, yet, on how to join together her flagrant freedom and self-respect with my inexperience and fear of God's punishment. We have been in conflict all day over whether or not to let Adam in when he finally arrives, but in the end, she insists we will spend time with him. He is the only man, so far, who has knowingly seen the Well-Woman and called her by name. Sadly, however, he has also kept his knowledge and love for the Well-Woman silent in his own life, and silence of this kind is not something the Well-Woman likes. Still, she wishes to see him.

He comes in. We sit and drink and talk; the three of us are together for several hours, this evening being the culmination of many months of resisting being together. Adam is easy with both the Well-Woman's passion and my relative innocence and is seemingly untroubled by our discord.

We enjoy our evening and will revel in thinking about it tomorrow, but during these hours with the three of us together, the Well-Woman begins to whisper her usual mantra to me. I hear it growing louder and louder as the night wears on.

I need to be seen. I need to be known. Speak. No more silences. No more secrets. No more hiding me. Do not accept this. Speak. Over and over she drawls out the words. I wonder, momentarily, if she isn't being greedy to expect so much speaking, so much forthrightness from me in every relationship. What I have with Adam is warm and interesting tonight. Isn't that enough? But I entertain these ideas only until midnight when, like Cinderella, the spell is broken, and the authentic identity of the beautiful maiden is restored.

When Adam finally goes away and the Well-Woman and I are alone into the early morning hours, she reminds me of the secrets and silences we have already suffered. Then she makes me bring to mind the relief, of late, of living truthfully. By the time I drift off to sleep, I am in agreement with her point of view that Adam cannot be allowed to keep our relationship secret.

I resolve to make several promises to the Well-Woman intended to cement our relationship. I will not compromise her determination to live out loud and to be seen.

I rise late the morning after the visit from our man. I collect the things I will need for a ceremony. Several weeks before, I purchased a ring that the Well-Woman noticed in a local gallery. I take this out of my jewelry box and put it into my knapsack, along with a thermos of Jasmine tea, an umbrella, and a portable CD player. I get into my new red car and drive us down to a park that looks across a lake and toward the city I live in and love. This park happens to be the very same place where my eighth grade graduation party was held so many years ago. I am pleased to be back here, reclaiming the wildishness I left behind in earnest that summer between junior high and high school when I "gave my life away to the Lord."

It takes me just a few moments to set up the elements needed for our ritual. It is raining, naturally, so the grief that has been so near to me of late is amply represented. I pour the tea into one cup only and sip slowly from it until I am warmed. The CD player gives off quiet tones of Benedictine chants as I settle on the park bench and dig out the ring and the vows we have written to one another. I take in the clean air, resting.

Finally, I feel prepared to make my promises and to receive the till-death-do-us-part devotion of the Well-Woman.

She speaks first, solemn but with the carefree self-confidence that is her central attraction for me. Her voice is clear, low, and lovely. *"I promise to guide you into places of health and truth and freedom. I will speak to you regarding issues of intimacy, taste, commitment, career, intellectual pursuits, and spirituality. I will be your connection to the Divine Shadow Figure and will dance on your behalf with the Shadow and with all who are willing to see me clearly. Depend on me. I have energy and wisdom and sensuality and clear eyes. I will go with you everywhere you go. I will embrace you in your sadness and defend you against your enemies, Pretending and Façade. I will be calm for you in every anxious moment."*

I listen to her words carefully. Breathe . . . breathe . . . My chest is clear. The rain ticks the top of the umbrella. The monks chant their otherworldly retort to the sound of traffic in the distance. After a few moments, I speak my vows in return.

"I promise to look toward your interests in every relationship I have," I begin. I am stopped here as the implications of such a promise crystallize in my imagination. This has already meant paying a great cost, and I foresee more expenses in the coming future. When I can, I go on. "I will speak the truths you whisper to me, listen to your voice on matters of intimacy, taste, commitments, career, intellectual pursuits, and spirituality." Again, I pause. These are not small commitments to be making for a lifetime. Am I sure I can live by them? Briefly, the alternative, my former way of being, comes to me, and I know this new partnership must be made permanent. I conclude with the most important vow I make this morning, "I promise to live my life on behalf of your health and peace of mind above that of anyone else." Have I ever put myself first before? This seems a frightening but necessary prospect, and now I have said it.

I breathe again and then take the ring, a thick, antique silver band with a stone the color of blood fastened in the center, I and slip it onto the ring finger of my right hand (not the finger of marriage commitments, but the place where a different sort of union will be displayed). I sip the tea and look out at the city sky-line.

We have come to the end of things being as they have been, my dear catalyst. I don't destroy the letters you wrote to me, nor do I revile the memory of our walk on the beach or our stolen moments. These may be your secrets but they are not secrets to me. They are songs to a powerful awakening.

CONCLUDING REMARKS

As I mentioned in the introduction, Dear Reader, these stories are meant to be examples of what *you* can do as you work with the parts of you that weigh in about what you are allowed to do in life, what ways you're allowed to be creative, what risks you're allowed to take.

To this day, I bump up against resistance and fear and anxiety that makes me hold my breath and wonder if I'll ever be completely free of the voices in my head. Fortunately, I now know how to have conversations with the parts of myself that hold unhelpful and damaging or constricting narratives and beliefs.

I want all of us to be able to be led into our creativity by the core self—the part that holds truth and wisdom! I hope you will take to the page. Right now. I hope you will open a document and let all of the parts of you have a voice, so they can be relieved of their pain. I am a strong believer that hating on aspects of the self is not the way to calm those aspects. Rather, listen. Listen and observe and then have conversations with your parts. In this way, you will become the leader of the voices that are now keeping you stuck.

And if you need or want support on this journey, you can find it here: www.thenarrativeproject.net.

ABOUT THE AUTHOR

Cami Ostman is a writing coach and life coach, author of *Second Wind: One Woman's Midlife Quest to Run Seven Marathons on Seven Continents*, and the co-editor of *Beyond Belief: The Secret Lives of Women in Extreme Religion* (Seal Press). Cami holds a Bachelor of Education in English and Theater from Western

Washington University and a Master of Science in Marriage and Family Therapy from Seattle Pacific University. She runs a nine-month program to help writers get their books done called The Narrative Project. She is also a dog lover, a wine connoisseur, a runner, and a blogger. Her blogs can be found at 7marathons7continents.com, and psychologytoday.com/blog/secondwind. Her professional offerings can be found at thenarrativeproject.net. Cami has been reviewed or featured in *O Magazine*, *Adventures Northwest*, *Fitness Magazine*, and *The Atlantic*. She lives in Seattle, Washington, with her four-legged creatures.